LANCE STAR
Sky Ranger

AIRSHIP 27 PRODUCTIONS

Airship 27 Presents
"LANCE STAR: Sky Ranger" Volume 4

"Ring of Fire" copyright © 2014 Bobby Nash
"The Devil's Arm Gambit" copyright © 2014 Andrew Salmon
"Black Cloud Ace" copyright © 2014 Jim Beard
"Die Like a Man" copyright © 2014 Sean Taylor

Lance Star is copyright © 2014 by Bobby Nash

Published by Airship 27 Productions
Airship27Hangar.com

Cover illustration copyright © 2014 Felipe Echevarria
Interior illustrations copyright © 2014 Scott P. "Doc" Vaughn

Editor: Ron Fortier
Associate Editor: Gordon Dymowski
Promotions and marketing manager: Michael Vance
Production and design: Rob Davis

Lance Star logo design by Matt Talbot

ISBN-13: 978-0-692-02220-7 (Airship 27)
ISBN-10: 069022201

Second Edition

Printed in the United States of America

10 9 8 7 6 5 4 3 2 1

Volume IV

⊹ *Lance Star* ⊹

"Ring of Fire"

by
Bobby Nash

It had started out as just another run.

What should have been a routine assignment had quickly devolved into a nightmare. The steering yoke jerked and jiggled in his hands, desperate to break free from its control column housing. It took all of the air ace's skill to hold it steady, but it was a constant struggle.

If he had been in the cockpit of the Skybolt things might have gone smoother, but the cargo plane was larger and far more bulky than the silver streak that often made the newsreels. By comparison, piloting the cargo plane was like flying a brick with wings. It was anything but easy.

Around them, all the pilot could see was thick, white clouds. Their instruments were all but useless in this soup so they were essentially flying blind. They had already hit something in the cloud cover and whatever it was it was big, so big, in fact, that it had sent the plane into a spin before Lance was able to regain control. One of the starboard engines flamed out immediately following the impact.

That's when the ride started to get really bumpy.

The second was already starting to sputter, but hadn't quite on them yet. The cargo plane dropped out of cloud cover and Lance was about to breathe a sigh of relief, but then realized that something wasn't right. They had been on course for a small ring of recently discovered islands in the South Pacific. They were still heading toward the crescent shaped cove that had been their destination, but it was far larger than the map they had been shown led them to believe.

He couldn't believe what he was seeing.

The clouds they had flown through had been white and clear, but beneath the fluffy cirrus clouds a thunderstorm was brewing. Grey, angry clouds roiled with thunder and lightning as it poured rain onto the island below.

"Hold on!" he shouted over his shoulder to the rest of the Sky Rangers, who were strapped to their seats long the sides of the cargo bay along with their guests and several cargo containers that were clamped down to the floor. Buck Tellonger sat to his right in the cockpit, acting as his co-pilot for this run. "I'm going to try and set her down!" he said.

"Where?" Buck shouted, but Lance could barely hear him over the cacophony of sounds echoing all around him.

"Your guess is as good as mine," he answered. "Find me a landing strip, Buck!"

"Are you kidding? I-- Look out!" Buck shouted a warning, but Lance had seen it too and was already acting. With deft precision, Lance maneuvered the cargo plane through the rush of large beasts that surrounded them. They looked like birds, but at the same time they didn't look like any bird he had ever laid eyes on in his life. Their wingspan was lengthy, some the size of small planes like the Sky Rangers own one-man sized Skeeters.

Buck took the plane into a roll, narrowing avoiding a collision with one of the creatures. Another dive and turn got them out of the way of another, but there was no way he would be able to dodge them all and keep the plane in the air. Lance was an exceptional pilot, but even he wasn't that good. Especially when he was one engine short.

"Hold on!" he shouted again and took the cargo plane into a steep dive, which took them out of the path of the giant birds. The plane began to shake and a sound like a rushing wave or a freight train overshadowed the sound of the plane's skin as it began to pull apart from stresses it was not designed to tolerate.

Once they were below the-- Lance didn't really have a word for the creatures he saw-- well, at least no word he would dare say aloud. Lance evened out their descent as best he could. The cargo plane had taken a beating and the rough ride had done a number on the rest of the Sky Rangers and their cargo. Lance knew he needed to put the plane on the ground fast.

The only problem was there didn't seem to be a single flat piece of ground on the entire island. The people they had been sent to meet had arrived by boat, but the radio message Lance had listened to mentioned a safe place to land. If there was a landing strip on the island it wasn't very easy to find.

"There!" Buck shouted and pointed. "Two O'clock."

Lance saw what his co-pilot had pointed out. It was a small open field, barely long enough to constitute a runway, but their options were rather limited. Beyond the field was a cliff with what appeared to be a long vertical drop to the ocean below. It was not the ideal landing site, but at the moment they had no other options.

"I see it, Buck!"

"Can you make that?"

Lance shrugged. "Do I have a choice?"

"Not really," Buck said. "It's either that or we go for a swim."

"I didn't bring my trunks," Lanced quipped.

"I guess you better keep it on dry land then, boss," Buck said.

"If you insist," Lance said with a smile. He touched the throat microphone at his neck so he could talk to the Sky Rangers in the cargo hold. "We're coming in for a landing, folks," Lance said. "It might be a bit bumpy so make sure everyone's strapped in good and snug."

Red Davis' voice rang in Lance's earphone receivers. He reported back that they were all strapped in and ready.

"Hold onto your socks, Buck," Lance said playfully. He was enjoying himself. "We're going in."

Lance took the plane into a turn and angled up on the clearing. He dropped the landing gear. He didn't realize that he had been holding his breath until after the landing wheels dropped from their housings.

The ground came up at the quickly until, even through the rain-streaked front windows they could pick out trees and other vegetation growing on the island. The pilots bounced around in their seats as the cargo plane scrubbed the tops of trees on its approach. There was nothing Lance could do about the trees because fighting the wind and rain was taking his full concentration.

"That ground is going to be soft from all this rain, Buck," he said. We mighty not stop in time."

"Not much we can do about it," Buck said as he chewed on one of his smelly, but thankfully unlit stogies. Lance had refused to smell those god-awful things all the way from New York to their destination south of the equator.

"I suppose not," Lance said and smiled. He clicked the throat mic. "We're down in five, people. Brace yourselves."

The wheels touched down on the muddy field and instantly sank in deep. The cargo plane's front went one way and the momentum of the descent sent the tail spinning around. Buck flipped off the engines just as they had touched ground, but there was no way to stop momentum. The plane slid through the mud, slowing only slightly after touchdown.

Lance kept his grip on the yoke even though he was no longer in control of the plane. Whether they stopped in time or not would be up to the big co-pilot in the sky. He just hoped the big guy was in a generous mood today.

The cliff grew closer even as their speed slowed. Through Buck's side window they could see the cliff getting nearer and nearer. Then they hit something that would have thrown both men from their seats if they had not been wearing their seat belts.

Their momentum stopped and the plane settled into the mud.

Everything was at a slight angle, but at least they were in one piece. Buck looked out the window and whistled. They were only inches away from the edge.

And it was a long drop to the rocks below.

Lance pulled off his helmet.

"Do I want to know how close we came?" he asked after hearing his co-pilot's whistle. He tucked the helmet into a pouch next to the pilot's seat.

"Nope," Buck said.

"I didn't think so."

Lance disconnected the throat mic from the control console, un-strapped himself, and headed aft to check on the others. It was only a few steps down to reach the cargo hold, which took up the majority of the plane's structure. The Sky Rangers were already up and about. Red was checking on the cables that held the cargo in place to make sure everything was secure. Cy Hawkins was making sure that all of the plane's systems were secure and that there was no chance of fire. Jim Nolan was taking care of their guests, Professor Farrington and his daughter Nicole.

"What the heck hit us?" Cy asked when he saw Lance approach. He was cranking open the rear cargo hatch manually since the plane was at an angle.

"You wouldn't believe me if I told you," Lance said as he followed Cy out of the hatch onto the ramp.

Cy stopped at the bottom and he looked up into the foreboding sky.

"You okay?" Lance asked as he stuffed the folded up throat mic into a zippered pocket on his left arm.

"Tell me that's not what I think it is," Cy said as he pointed skyward.

"Told you it was unbelievable," Lance said as he watched the prehistoric birds soar over the downed cargo plane. He wished he had a camera on board. No one back home was going to believe this one.

"Is that what we hit?"

"Afraid so, Cy," Buck said as he joined them on the ramp. Rainwater poured off the roof of the plane and was quickly filling the ditch the plane's landing created with muddy water.

"But that's... I mean, how is that here?" Cy asked.

"Search me," Lance said as he watched the pterodactyls, for really they couldn't have been anything else, with astonishment. "Look at the wings on that thing. They're massive."

"Incredible," Nicole Farrington said as she joined them, holding her father's left arm. Jim Nolan was on the opposite side, helping the older man keep his balance.

"This is amazing," Professor Farrington said. "Simply amazing."

"That seems to be the general consensus, Professor," Lance said. "My question is where did they come from? Even more importantly, where is the rest of your team?"

"Look at how they move," Farrington said. "So graceful. More like a bird than I would have thought possible."

"I just hope those big suckers don't get the idea that we're worms down here in the mud," Red Davis joked.

"I doubt that's the case," the professor said.

"Just to be on the safe side, have one of those rifles ready in case those big birds get hungry," Buck whispered to Red, who nodded and went to the weapons locker to retrieve it.

"I've seen dryer monsoons than this, boss," Cy Hawkins said.

Lance was about to reply when the rain stopped as if a switch had been flipped. A sliver of sunlight cut through the ominous gray clouds above seconds later and suddenly the island took on a completely different hue. The light hitting the trees and mountain nearly glowed in comparison to the dark background of the sky. It made everything look odd, almost fake.

"This must be what's it's like to land on another planet," Red Davis muttered.

Cy gave him a strange look and shook his head. He never could understand his friend's fascination with those science fiction pulp rags that told unbelievable stories about traveling to other planets or going back in time to the time of the dinosaurs. Then again, he had just watched a flock of pterodactyls, creatures that were supposed to have gone extinct several million years earlier so he guessed if that was possible, then perhaps one day man might just make the journey into outer space.

"We've got incoming," Buck said, drawing Cy's attention back to the problem at hand.

Lance instinctively dropped a hand to his sidearm, but did not pull it when he saw what Buck was referring to. Two covered trucks were driving across the rough terrain headed straight toward them.

"Professor Thornby?" he asked.

"That would be my assumption, yes," the professor said. "It is my understanding that this island is uninhabited, with the exception of our science team. Professor Thornby was appraised of our arrival time and was set to meet us."

"Let's go say hello, then. Professor, wait here while Buck and I greet our guests." Lance stepped off the ramp into the thick squishy mud--

And immediately sank to his ankles.

It took a small amount of effort, but he was able to walk away from the torn up patch off ground their landing had created. By the time the trucks reached them Lance and Buck were on solid ground to meet them. Everyone else remained aboard the plane until Lance gave the word that it was safe.

Hand still on the butt of his gun, Lance approached the passenger side door. A stocky man dropped to the ground in front of him, a big smile plastered across his face, his rosy nose almost matched the bright shade of his cheeks.

"Professor Thornby?" Lance asked.

"That would be me," the clean-shaven cherub faced professor said with a deep, operatic voice. "I assume you are Mister Star?"

"That's right." Lance stuck out a hand and the professor shook it heartily. Once he released his grip, Lance motioned toward Buck, who was chewing on an unlit cigar nearby. "This is my Chief Officer, Buck Tellonger."

"Pleased to meet you," Buck said and also shook hands with the man.

"Looks like you had a bit of trouble on the way in," Thornby said while staring at the plane that was partially buried in the mud at such an odd angle.

"You could say that," Buck joked.

"Are our supplies intact?" Thornby asked excitedly. "And was Professor Farrington able to make the trip?"

"He's onboard," Lance said. "So is your cargo."

"Excellent." Thornby rubbed his hands together like an excited schoolboy.

"We're fine too, by the way," Buck muttered. If the professor heard him, he didn't feel the need to comment.

"If you and your men can give us a hand," Lance continued. "We'll get the supplies loaded on your truck and you can give us a ride to your camp."

"Of course, Mister Star, but we must hurry."

"Are you expecting another storm?"

"Actually, yes, we are," Thornby said. "But on this island, gentlemen, it isn't the storm you have to worry about."

"Oh?" Buck asked, suddenly even more concerned.

"It's what the storm brings you have to worry about."

⊥

The road, for lack of a better term, was bumpy.

The Sky Rangers rode in the back of the second truck as it bounced along the rough-worn path on the way to Professor Thornby's base camp. It had taken a good twenty minutes of driving over uneven terrain filled with deep ruts and gouges to arrive, but they made it safely and without incident, if not comfortably. While Buck supervised the unloading of the supplies in conjunction with the professor's men, Lance accompanied Thornby, Farrington, and his daughter to the main tent. Jim Nolan came along. In addition to having an interest in archaeology, it was clear that Jim had also developed a particular interest in Nicole Farrington. Not that Lance could blame him. She was quite the looker and she seemed to enjoy the attention the pilot was paying her way.

"Does your radio work?" Lance asked once they were inside. He pointed toward a small table in one corner with a beat up old radio set up that looked like it had seen better days.

"Intermittent at best, I'm afraid," Thornby informed him as if radio contact with the outside world wasn't all that important. "There's some kind of naturally occurring phenomenon that blocks radio transmissions onto or off of the island. We've been trying to figure it out, but so far we're drawing a blank."

"Could it be caused by the dense cloud cover we flew through to get here?" Lance asked. "It was pretty turbulent and surrounded the entire island. We weren't truly sure it was here until we broke through."

"It could be. Our best guess is that the interference has something to do with the cloud cover," Thornby said. "However, it's not a cloud per se."

"What is it?" Jim Nolan asked.

"Smoke. Perhaps mixed with a bit of fog and ash."

"I beg your pardon?" Jim asked.

"The cloud cover is made up of smoke and volcanic ash."

"Volcanic ash?" Lance asked.

"Yes."

"I know I'm going to regret asking, but where would volcanic ash come from?"

"The volcano."

"See, I knew you were going to say that." Lance wanted to smack the man. He held up a finger, but bit back on the angry retort he wanted to shout. He reigned in his annoyance. At least a little bit.

"Then why did you ask?" Thornby said without glancing in the pilot's direction.

"Look, mister, I'm not one of your students. Now you'd better start giving me some straight answers or I'm going to..."

"Mister Star," Professor Farrington said loudly. It was the first time he'd heard the man raise his voice. "Decorum, please."

"My apologies, Professor," Lance said, lowering his voice back to normal levels. "Now, perhaps you should start from the beginning."

Thornby sighed then turned to face the pilots with a look that had probably intimidated many a student. "This island is situated right at the heart of the Ring of Fire. Are you at all familiar with the Ring of Fire, Mister Star?"

"Not really."

Thornby sidled into teaching mode. He stepped over to a map taped to the tent's canvas. "The Pacific Ocean is surrounded by a zone of violent volcanic and earthquake activity in this area here." He circled a large area on the map with his finger before tapping the center of the circle where the island where they now stood was located. "Scientists refer to this area as the Ring of Fire."

"Active volcanic activity?" Jim asked.

"Yes," Professor Farrington said before Thornby could continue. "The Ring is subject to tropical cyclones, typhoons, tropical cyclones, hurricanes, fog, and other nautical hazards."

"That's a pretty big area."

"Yes. Most of the time this area is relatively safe, Mister Star," he said. "Although, as I'm sure you understand, there are always dangers out on the open seas."

Lance nodded.

"We have made some amazing strides in the fields of seismology and volcanology, but no matter how far we've come in our understanding we cannot effectively predict earthquakes nor volcanic eruptions before they happen," Thornby interjected. "Perhaps one day that will change and we can pinpoint the early warning signs to predict them. Or better yet, find a way to correct for geologic instability and stop these devastating events from occurring in the first place."

"You really think you can do that?" Jim Nolan asked, clearly intrigued by the notion.

"Someday, perhaps," Thornby said with a shrug. "If that day comes, and I pray it does, it will be thanks in no small part to the work we are doing here."

"I don't follow," Lance said. "How does an archaeological dig on this island help you predict a volcano erupting? Unless..."

"You've guessed correctly, Mister Star," Thornby said before the air ace could finish. "This island is not actually an island in the strictest sense of the word. It is actually the peak of a very large, and very active, volcano."

"You can't be serious," Lance said.

"Oh yes, I can," Thornby said proudly. "In fact, right now we are standing at the center of the volcano's crater."

Lance Star woke to a familiar sound.

The discussion—okay, it was an argument—he'd had with Professor Thornby after learning the true nature of the island they had landed upon had taken a lot out of him. Had he known that this place was actually a live volcano that could probably erupt any day, he might have thought twice about accepting the job of piloting Professor Farrington and his supplies. Okay, that was a lie. Lance was first and foremost an adventurer. Like every one of the Sky Rangers, he was a natural born thrill-seeker. And despite his protestations to the contrary to Thornby, this place was no different than the time they traveled to Kun Lun or that hidden village in the Alps or any of the other adventures they'd undertaken.

After he said his piece, which hadn't swayed the professor one iota, one of Thornby's assistants showed him to the guest tent where the pilots would be staying while they were guests of Professor Thornby's expedition. Jim agreed to head back to the truck and fill in Buck and the others on what was going on and then help Miss Farrington stow her and her father's gear in their tent.

Lance was exhausted. He hadn't planned on taking a nap, but once he sat on the cot and got comfortable, his body informed him that it had other plans. He was asleep seconds later.

He wasn't sure how long he had been out when the familiar whine of a plane's engine snapped him back to reality. He sat up on the cot in the guest tent and listened. For a moment he thought he'd imagined it, but then he heard the unmistakable thrum of an engine passing by overhead.

Normally, the sound of an airplane engine soothed him and he wouldn't have thought twice about waking to the sound. There were many a morning when he awoke in his bungalow at Star Field and just lay in bed and listen to the sound of the planes being worked on nearby. There was nothing as soothing to him as the purr of a well-timed engine firing on all cylinders.

Today, however, the sound felt out of place.

Lance ran out into the blinding sunlight. It took his eyes a moment to adjust to the glare. When it did he noticed that the other pilots had a similar idea. Lance scanned the skies above looking for the source of the sound.

"Do you see it?" Cy Hawkins asked.

"Not yet," Buck Tellonger answered.

"There!" Red Davis pointed and all eyes followed his finger toward the spot.

Shading his watering eyes with his hands, Lance strained to see what his oldest friend was pointing toward. It didn't take long for him to find it. A squadron of six planes, two-seaters from the look of them, approached from the north end of the island heading south.

Seconds after he caught sight of them, the planes flew over Professor Thornby's camp. They were flying low, maybe one hundred feet above the hard deck. Maybe even a little lower. Flying close to the deck took skill. Whoever they were, these pilots had skill.

That's when Lance recognized the all too familiar emblem emblazoned on the rear fuselage of the closest plane.

And his blood ran cold.

"Nazis," he whispered as he watched them fly off into the distance. From their trajectory and angle of descent, Lance was certain that they were coming in for a landing on the island and that could only mean one thing.

"We've got trouble, boss," Buck Tellonger said as he ran to Lance's side.

"Yeah," Lance said. "I see 'em."

"What do you think they want?"

"Whatever it is, it can't be good."

"You'll get no argument from me on that score," Buck said.

"Buck, make sure everyone is wearing their sidearm and check the perimeter. I don't want those bastards trying to sneak in here without us knowing they're coming."

"You got it."

Lance started toward the main tent.

"Where will you be?" Buck asked.

"I'm going to have a little chat with our host."

"Nazis," he whispered...

"What do you mean, you're not worried about it?"

Lance Star couldn't believe what he was hearing. He'd burst into the main tent like a wild man, telling the assembled scientists about the squadron of Nazi planes that had just buzzed their camp. He wasn't sure what to expect. The news of Nazi fighter planes in the area usually elicited panic, fear, and most often a desire to put as much distance between yourself and the newcomers.

The Sky Rangers had crossed paths with Nazis before and at no time had any of those encounters ended well. Generally, they concluded with guns blazing or punches being thrown. Although there was no official declaration of war between the Axis Powers and the United States of America, Lance was among a growing number of Americans that felt like it was only a matter of time before the Nazis and their partners turned their eye toward the USA. A second World War was imminent.

Professor Thornby shrugged as if the arrival of the worst villains of the modern era were no big deal. "We are aware of their presence, Mister Star," he said. "The Germans have a camp in a cove at the southernmost edge of this island."

Lance leaned forward, his hands balled into fists on the makeshift table full of pieces the archaeological team had dug up recently. He was incensed. "You mean to tell me that you knew there were enemy agents on this island and you didn't feel it was worth mentioning?"

"Enemy agents?" Thornby shook his head in a dismissive manner. Lance had seen this same gesture from many an academic when they decided not to deal with real world issues practically. College professors were the worst. "The last time I checked, Mister Star, the United States of America was not at war with Germany," Thornby continued.

"Not yet, at least," Lance added angrily. He pointed in the general direction he'd seen the planes go. "You can't tell me that once these guys finish ravaging Europe they're just going to stop, can you? It's just a matter of time until they set their sights on the good ol' U. S. of A, gentlemen."

"And when that day comes then I will worry about it, Mister Star. I refuse to treat these men like monsters without hard evidence."

"Hard..." Lance was speechless. He wanted to argue the point, but he had met men like Thornby before. He was close minded and would not listen to any point of view that did not match his own. Arguing with him would be a pointless gesture and a complete waste of time.

"Besides, when I spoke with their commander a couple of days ago, he promised me that they were not interested in our work and that they would not interfere with our work as long as we afforded them the same courtesy."

"Wait," Lance said, his jaw hanging open. "You spoke to him? He was here?"

"Yes. The commander of the expedition and I had a nice, pleasant chat right out there." He pointed toward the table and chairs under the tent's awning. "We promised not to bother one another."

"Oh, he promised, did he?"

"Yes he did. And I fully intend to uphold my end of the bargain, Mister Star," Thornby said with more than a hint of aggravation that made his already cherry tinted cheeks glow a little brighter. He was probably used to getting his way when it came to his students, but Lance had dealt with the Nazis before. Experience told him that they could not be trusted.

Lance turned on his heel and headed toward the exit.

"Don't do anything stupid, Mister Star," Thornby called out from behind.

Lance bit back a scathing retort and kept walking, pushing aside the tent flap angrily. This time the sudden glare was a welcome change of scenery.

"What's the plan, Lance?" Buck asked. He had obviously been waiting outside the tent. As instructed, he was wearing his pistol in a holster on his belt. He had another belt and gun held in his hand and passed them over to Lance.

"Thornby's not willing to listen to reason," Lance said as he put on the belt and adjusted the holster on his hip. "He doesn't think the Nazis are a problem at the moment."

"Doesn't sound very smart of him," Buck said.

"Agreed." Lance fastened the belt buckle. "Not much I can do about him at the moment. Right now we're stuck here."

"Not a very tenable position, I admit."

"No it's not, Buck. Our first priority is to find a way off this island."

"Agreed."

"Take Red and Jim back to the plane and let's see if we can get her dug out and ready to fly," Lance said. "Just in case this goes sideways and we need to leave in a hurry."

"You got it." Buck started to walk away, but stopped. So, uh, what exactly are you planning to do in the meantime?" he asked.

Lance smiled. "I thought Cy and I might go for a little hike. We need to survey the area for volcanic activity so we might as well get on that right away."

"Starting at the southern tip, no doubt."

Lance's smile widened. "Why, Buck, you read my mind."

Lance and Cy had been walking for an hour.

They had caught a ride with Buck and the others as far as the cargo plane. While the other Sky Rangers got to work on digging out the plane from the mud where they had landed. Buck and the guys had a bit of work ahead of them, but Lance knew they could manage. He just hoped that the plane hadn't sustained any serious damage in the landing.

Lance and Cy had commented several times during their walk about how surprisingly flat the land was here.

"I wonder what happened to those..." Cy started, but trailed off.

"Those what?"

"You know. Those things we saw overhead when we got here." He flapped his hand with the thumb and pinky stretched out like wings.

"You mean the pterodactyls?" Lance said around a grin.

"Those weren't pterodactyls," Cy exclaimed bluntly.

"What would you call them?"

"I don't know," Cy admitted. "But I damn sure wouldn't call them pterodactyls. Those things have been extinct for a long, long time, Boss. You know what they do to pilots that claim to see strange things like spaceships or flying dinosaurs?"

"No. What?"

"They lock them up in little rooms with padded walls and don't let them fly anymore, that's what."

"You're being ridiculous, Cy. We all saw the same thing."

"Hey, you go ahead and say you saw whatever you saw," Cy said and dismissed the notion of sharing this little secret with the world. "And I'll stop by and visit you in whatever nuthouse they lock you up in."

Lance laughed at his friend's cynical view of things. Then again, he couldn't completely dismiss Cy's logic either. Hadn't he also dismissed people as kooks whenever he heard of a UFO sighting? Was claiming to see supposedly extinct prehistoric animals any different?

They walked the next mile or so in silence, each of them scanning the sky and the mountain ranges for sight of the winged creatures, whatever they might be. So far they hadn't seen a trace of them.

"It sure is beautiful here," Cy finally said. "Reminds me a bit of home, actually. You know, except for the ocean being so close. Not a lot of oceans nearby when I was growing up." Cy had grown up on a farm that was surrounded on all sides by other farms. He was accustomed to flat vistas that stretched for miles whereas Lance was a born and bred New York boy who missed rolling hills and tall buildings that stretched into the sky.

Of course, once Lance explained that they were essentially standing in the middle of a volcano, Cy's view of the island dimmed a bit.

But only a bit.

"You think it's safe?"

"Both Thornby and Farrington seem to think so."

"Do you believe them?"

"I don't know," Lance said. "Farrington's a straight shooter so I trust him. Thornby is the one I'm not so sure about. Regardless, if and when this thing decides to blow its stack I don't want to be anywhere near it."

"Amen to that, Boss."

"If Buck can't get the plane ready then we're going to need to come up with an alternate mode of travel. Thornby has a boat, and that will do in a pinch, but it'll be a tight fit for all of us."

"Maybe one of the Ratzi's will loan us a plane or two?" Cy joked.

"Yeah," Lance chuckled. "That'll be the day."

"Speaking of which, why do you think the Nazi's are here?"

"I have no idea, Cy, but I don't trust them."

"Who does?"

"Thornby."

"Really?" Cy couldn't hide his surprise.

"Yeah. Apparently some big muckity muck Nazi commander told him they were here doing some scientific research and that they had no interest in what Thornby was doing."

"And he believed him?"

"Yeah," Lance said with a shake of his head. "Thornby's an academic. He doesn't see the real world the way those of us who live in it do."

"But still, he's trusting a Nazi," Cy said. "That can't ever be considered a good idea, can it?"

"You're preaching to the choir, partner," Lance said. "When it comes to big bad villains, the Nazis are right up there at the top of my list. I've met more than my fair share and I've yet to meet one that wasn't trying to kill me so..."

"I hear you. I just wish I knew what they were up to."

"That's why we're taking this little stroll," Lance reminded him as they climbed an embankment. "Careful now. We're close."

The ocean roared loudly nearby as the sound of waves crashing onto the shore echoed off the rocks. The two Sky Rangers crouched at the top of the rise and looked over the edge at the beach far below. The beach was nestled in a cove with a sheer cut half-moon shaped rock wall that offered the ideal natural perimeter fencing. The ocean covered the side not protected by the hardened lava and red clay compacted over centuries of volcanic eruptions.

Lance had little doubt that there was a German U-Boat or submarine somewhere out there, but the fog and cloud cover mix that obscured the island from the outside also made looking outward from the island just as difficult.

The Nazi planes were parked just off the beach on a hard packed clay field just large enough to accommodate a makeshift airstrip and a small prefabricated building placed nearby. Both of the Sky Rangers had seen planes of similar design before, but never on the ground. It was an odd sensation. Tents similar to those used by Thornby and his people were set up near the ridge, which provided a natural windbreak. Even Lance had to agree that it was a nice set up.

On the opposite side of the cove from the tents and planes were a series of camouflaged nets held up by poles at least fifteen to twenty feet tall. The net would effectively hide whatever was underneath from an aerial view.

From their vantage point, neither Lance nor Cy could make out what was beneath the netting. "I can't get a good line of sight on it," Lance said. "Can you?"

Cy looked through the binoculars. "No. I see movement, shadows, but not a clear view."

"Damn," Lance muttered.

"What do you think they're up to down there, Boss?"

"I don't know," Lance said. "But I bet it's nothing good."

"Agreed. So... closer look?"

Lance smiled. "Am I that easy to read?"

"Well," Cy said, dragging out the syllables. "Let's just say that I know you too well."

Lance clapped his friend on the shoulder.

"Come on. Let's find a way down," he said.

⊥

Getting down wasn't easy. Not that either of them had expected it to be. It was slow going, but eventually Lance and Cy found a path that was manageable considering that they had no climbing gear with them. The going was slow and treacherous. There were faster and easier ways down, but stealthy they weren't so they stuck to the out of the way path.

When they finally reached the bottom, the Sky Rangers found a spot to rest in a crevice behind a boulder that sat near the ridge wall. It wasn't overly roomy, but there was enough space for both of them to squeeze in and get, well, comfortable wasn't the right word, but at least they were out of sight.

The first tremor caught them off guard.

A rumble came from somewhere deep beneath them. It was so loud that it hurt their ears. The ground shook so hard that stones danced around atop the soil. The quake lasted all of two minutes, each of which seemed to last forever. The entire time, Lance kept an eye on the sky to the north, which was unfortunately partially blocked by the cliff face he and Cy had just climbed down. He let out a breath when he didn't see smoke and ash shooting skyward.

"What the hell was that?" Cy demanded, trying to keep his voice a whisper.

"That was trouble," Lance said. "Big trouble."

"You want to head back?"

"Not yet. We're here. We might as well take a look around."

"Spoken like a true crazy man," Cy noted.

Lance choked back a giggle.

"That wasn't a denial, boss."

"Something's not right here," Lance muttered, scratching his chin and feeling the couple of days worth stubble growing there.

"No kidding," Cy snorted. "We've got a volcanic island that could erupt at any time, mysterious flying critters that are supposed to be extinct, and God only knows what else is on this island. Oh yeah, and did I mention Nazis? And lest I forget, we've also got no way to get a radio signal off the island. We're flying blind on this one, boss. I'd say there's a whole lot of not right going on around here."

Lance chuckled in spite of himself. Cy's complaints were his way of reminding Lance of the precarious nature of their current situation. Lance realized that he was prone to diving headlong into danger, sometimes without a second thought as to the consequences. Despite that, he also knew that his team had his back, just as he had theirs. The Sky Rangers were more than a team. They were a band of brothers. Cy was reminding him just how outnumbered they were.

"The million dollar question is what are the Nazis doing here?"

"A good question, boss," Cy said. "But if it's all the same to you I'd rather have this conversation somewhere else. Maybe outside of weapon's range?"

Lance ignored Cy's cynicism. The former crop-duster liked to complain, but like the rest of the Sky Rangers, Cy Hawkins also enjoyed the adventure that came with wearing the Sky Ranger patch.

"Pirates, maybe?" Lance asked

"Pirates?" Cy asked. "As in '*yo, ho, ho and shiver me timbers*'? Those kind of pirates?"

Lance shrugged. "Why not?"

"Boy, we sure can pick 'em, can't we?"

"That's what makes our job so much fun, Cy," Lance reminded him.

"Right. Fun."

"What do you make of that?" Lance asked, pointing toward the camouflaged netting.

"I don't know. I saw movement so I know somebody is in there doing something."

"I saw that too," Lance muttered. "It's damn curious."

"What do you think they're up to under there?" Cy asked.

"Beats me," Lance said as he strained to see what was happening in the shadows of the camouflaged netting. "But I know Nazis. These guys are always up to something and it's generally no good."

"You'll get no argument from me, Boss."

For all of the planes and structures on this stretch of beach, there weren't a lot of people scurrying about. There was movement from beneath the netting. Curiosity gnawed at Lance's gut. He'd never been able to ignore a mystery. Even as a kid, he had to unlock every door, open every box, and always ask questions. His father had instilled a sense of adventure in young Lance. That feeling only grew once he was old enough to accompany Landon Star on one of his fabled adventures as they traveled around the world looking for one hidden treasure or another.

It was at times like these that Lance really missed his dad. Landon would have loved exploring this hidden island and all of its mysteries. He would've done so with a big smile on his face.

"I'm heading in for a closer look," Lance said.

"Are you nuts? We should be getting out of here. Why do you need to get closer?"

"How else am I going to get a better look?" Lance broke from cover and sprinted toward the closest edge of the netting where he stopped and knelt behind the cover of the bunched up netting and some large oil drums.

"Here we go again," Cy said once he was sure that no alarm sounded. He blew out a deep breath and wondered why he hadn't volunteered to stay and work on repairs before following his commander's lead and sprinting across the open beach. He joined Lance behind the oil drums. He too was curious what the Nazis were up to and some of the answers they sought would be on the other side of the netting.

Lance lifted the edge of the net and rolled under.

Cy followed suit.

There was very little light in the makeshift tent. A few stray beams of light filtered through the gaps and holes in the net, but it was still pretty dark. Neither of them had a flashlight handy. The makeshift tent was filled with metal. It took a second, but Lance finally realized that they were cages. Large cages.

"They wouldn't?" Cy said. He ran a hand along one of the solid steel bars on one of the empty cages. "Even these idiots aren't dumb enough to try and poach those things, are they?"

"You tell me," Lance said. He pointed toward three cages that were not empty. The occupants of the cages seemed to be asleep. Or drugged. They were the same creatures they had run into in the storm.

"Oh... my..." Cy said.

"Pretty impressive, aren't they?"

"I'll say. How can these... uh..." Cy struggled with saying the word out loud.

"Pterodactyls," Lance whispered. "As impossible as it seems, the Nazis are here hunting pterodactyl."

"But why?"

"I have no idea." Lance scratched his head. "I do know one thing though. Whatever they're up to, it can't be good."

"Oh, I don't know about that, Mister Star," a booming voice called out from the shadows.

Lance and Cy spun toward the sound, each reaching for their side arms. They weren't fast enough. Instead, the pilots found themselves staring down the barrels of several automatic weapons pointed directly at them. They froze their hands hovering mere centimeters away from the weapons holstered on their hips.

"I wouldn't do that if I were you," a smiling Nazi said from the shadows, clicking his tongue as a warning against pulling their guns.

Neither of the pilots was against trying to fight their way out, but they were outnumbered so Lance pulled his hand away from his holster. "Stand down, Cy," he said.

His partner complied.

As one of the soldiers relieved them of their weapons, a Nazi officer strode from the shadows wearing a full dress uniform that looked out of place on an island of prehistoric creatures. His medals were shined to perfection. He walked with his hands positioned behind his back and carried himself with a regal bearing, not an uncommon characteristic of most of the German officers Lance Star had met in his life. It was painfully obvious to all that this man was in charge.

"I am Major Wilhelm Adler, gentlemen," he said. "You are now my prisoners."

Buck Tellonger closed his eyes and hoped for the best.

With the help of Jim Nolan and Red Davis, they had managed to dig the plane's wheels out of the dried mud and get it situated on more or less flat ground. A detailed inspection showed very little damage to the plane's structure outside of the fact that one of the engines was inoperable after that midair collision with one of those flying beasts they had seen. They were already motivated, but the ground tremor they felt earlier had only added to their resolve to get repairs completed quickly.

Buck had seen a lot of strange things since joining the Sky Rangers and he knew what Lance said those creatures were, but he couldn't bring himself to think of them as dinosaurs. There had to be some other explanation.

Not that it mattered at the moment.

At the moment, Buck's thoughts were firmly on the inner workings of the airplane behind whose controls he now sat. Red and Jim had made some minor repairs to compensate for the missing engine. All that remained was to make sure the plane's engines worked.

He pulled the choke and pressed the ignition switch. The starter whirred and clicked a few times before the rotors began to spin, slowly at first, but then faster and faster until...

Ignition!

"That's my girl!" Buck shouted as he ran a hand over the console. "Red, get up here!"

"You bellowed?" Red Davis asked good-natured as he poked his head through the cockpit door.

"Strap yourself in."

As Red slid into the co-pilot's chair, Jim Nolan poked his head in. "Where we headed?" he asked.

"Red and I are going to do some recon," Buck said. "See if we can get a bead on Lance and Cy. They've been gone a little too long for my liking."

"And me?" Jim asked.

"I want you to hightail it back to camp. Make sure we've got sufficient landing room. I want to park this bucket as close as we can get it."

"You expecting trouble?"

"You know me, Jim," Buck said as he clamped a fresh cigar between his teeth. "I'm always expecting trouble. That's why I'm--"

"Never disappointed," the three of them said in unison, repeating one of Buck's favorite phrases.

"Exactly," Buck said with a grin. "Not get a move on. I don't want to spend any more time on this rock than I have to."

"Good luck and be careful," Jim said before making his way out of the plane and sealing the hatch behind him.

"See you back at camp," Red added.

"You ready?" Buck asked.

"All indicators show green," Red said. "We're good to go."

"Then we're gone," Buck said and pushed the throttle forward.

Seconds later, the cargo plane was climbing high into the air.

"And what do you think of our little island, Mister Star?"

When the Nazi major had told him that he and Cy were his prisoners, Lance had expected that, at best, they would be tossed inside one of the cages or, at worst, beaten or simply shot right then and there.

What he hadn't expected was to be sitting on a small deck off of the prefabricated building the Nazi officer used as his office sipping tea and watching the tide roll in. He had to admit that the cove the Germans and their playmates had taken as their base was lovely. Not only was it defensibly sound, but there was no beating that view.

He hadn't seen Cy since they were captured. The major told him that the other pilot was going to be detained, but not harmed. Lance wanted to believe it, but he had trouble taking the word of a Nazi.

"That's my girl!"

"Well, I have to admit that what little I've seen has been rather interesting," Lance said. He kept his mood light and friendly, as if sitting on a friend's deck sipping on a beer while waiting for a couple of steaks to cook up on the grill. Playing it smart, Lance hoped that a friendly chat would provide him with a few answers.

"Thank you," Adler said, clearly pleased with his small slice of heaven. "I find that if you take a few of the comforts of home with you when you travel it eases the pain of being so far from your home and family."

"Makes sense," Lance agreed. "Although, being a city boy, I'm used to a more stable footing. I could live without the ground tremors."

"An unavoidable blemish on an otherwise beautiful landscape," Adler commented. "But that's neither here nor there. What is it that brings you to this remarkable place so far from your little airport in New York, Mister Star?"

Little...? Lance bristled, but didn't take the bait. Although he had never met Adler before, the major was a lot like other Nazis he'd run across in his travels. He was smug and arrogant, but also intelligent. His actions so far confirmed that he was a cunning strategist.

Lance took a sip of his tea while he reigned in his anger. "Oh, you know how it is, Major," he said. "The Sky Rangers are explorers. We like a good adventure so when Professor Thornby, I believe you've met him, yes..."

"Yes," Adler said. "The professor and I had a lovely chat shortly after I arrived. A lovely gentleman, although somewhat lacking in the social graces."

"Brother, you said a mouthful," Lance said. "But, yeah. That's him. Anyway, his people at the university hired us to make a supply run and here we are."

Adler leaned back comfortably in the chair, although his posture retained its rigid quality. "Honestly?" he asked.

Lance held up the middle three fingers of his right hand. "Scout's honor," he said.

Adler leaned forward, his posture more businesslike than before. "I have heard of you, Mister Star."

"One of the downsides of fame," Lance quipped. "No matter where I go, everybody seems to know my name."

"Indeed. I can see how that might prove a hindrance. Especially in your line of work."

"My line of work?"

"Yes. Espionage is not a profession where fame is an asset, Mister Star."

Lance laughed. "I agree. Lucky for me I'm a pilot and not a spy then, huh? Personally, you can bag all the fame and celebrity and drop it down the nearest hole, but I have to admit that it does help keep business rolling in. People see us in the newsreels and it brings business right to our door. Star Cargo Freight probably brings in most of the profit for my company. People are fascinated with air travel and the machines that allow us to soar above the clouds. There's a mystique that many, especially those who have never left the ground, find romantic. Of course, you probably know this, what with you being a pilot yourself."

He pointed toward the major's medals.

"From what I see there it looks like you're a rather good at it too."

"Yes. I am," Adler said, a thin proud smile creasing his otherwise stoic features. "The Luftwaffe only accepts the best."

"I'll bet," Lance said. "Who knows, Major. In another time, another place, you and me, we could've done some business together. Maybe even been drinking buddies had things worked out differently. You know, that whole conquer the world BS your Fuehrer has been spouting."

Adler chuckled. "Did you know that the exploits of Lance Star and his mighty Sky Rangers have reached all the way to Berlin? It's true."

"I can't say I did," Lance said. "I suppose I should be flattered." This time he sat casually instead of matching the major's posture. He understood that their pleasant conversation was actually a battle of wits. Others had described this type of verbal sparing as something akin to a chess match, but Lance preferred to think of it more like an intense poker game. Lance was a master at the poker table. In poker, it didn't always matter what hand he was holding. In poker, the cards were secondary. The best players were the ones who played the man across from him. Knowing how your opponent thinks and acts is just as important as the cards dealt. Lance was employing a similar strategy here with Major Adler, who seemed to know a thing or two about the game himself.

"It is true," Adler continued. "I have read various reports of your exploits. And, of course, I have seen you and your Sky Rangers on the American newsreels. They do so enjoy showing footage of your famous plane, don't they?"

"I suppose."

"And indeed they should, Mr. Star. The Skybolt, is a beautiful feat of engineering. You should be very proud of it."

"I am. I'll let my staff know you're pleased with their work."

"It is a shame you did not bring your famous aircraft on this trip. I would have appreciated the opportunity to get a closer look at it."

"Maybe next time."

"Perhaps." Adler's predatory smile widened. "At any rate, I have enjoyed hearing of your adventures."

"I'm flattered, I guess. Hopefully, you're hearing the good stuff," he said and smiled.

"That depends on your point of view, I would assume," Adler said. "I do have a couple of colleagues who told me that they had met you."

"Oh?"

"I believe you know Baron Von Blood, yes?"

"Otto? Oh yeah, me and Otto go way back," Lance said as if he and the baron were old friends, which couldn't be farther from the truth. Baron Otto Von Blood was an Austrian Air Ace that the Sky Rangers had crossed paths with on a number of occasions. One of those encounters resulted in the death of young Skip Terrel and the wounding of Walt Anderson. Although Walt retained the use of his leg, his days in the cockpit were over. Lance offered Walt a new challenge, running the day to day operations of Lance Star, Inc. Walt took to the job with gusto and thrived. Under his direction, Lance's business had better profits than ever.

Lance had made a promise to Betty that he would kill the man who took her brother from them. It was a promise he intended to keep.

Major Adler reminded Lance a little of Baron Von Blood. They both carried themselves in a way that suggested he was the most important person in the room. Lance had heard rumors that the baron had joined up with the Nazis, but Adler's admission that they knew one another confirmed it.

"And how is old Otto these days?" Lance asked.

"He was well the last time I saw him," Adler said. "Perhaps you would like me to relay a message to him the next time I see him?"

Lance pursed his lips then harrumphed. "Just... uh.... just tell him I've been looking forward to seeing him again. How about that?"

"I shall pass that along after I return to Berlin," Adler said. "But for now, I think you and I should dismiss with the pleasantries and, how do you Americans say it, get down to business, no?"

"I'd say it's well past time," Lance said, still sitting comfortably. "What are you doing here, Major?"

"I asked you first, Mister Star."

"And I told you," Lance said, allowing a hint of irritation creep into his voice. "I'm here making a cargo run to Professor Thornby's expedition.

That's all. Nothing else."

Major Adler let out a derisive snort. "Do you honestly expect me to believe that it is a coincidence that one of the United States' top operatives is simply delivering cargo to this particular island and this particular time?"

"Top operative?" Lance couldn't believe his ears. He also couldn't keep the look of surprise off of his face. "You must have me confused with somebody else, Major. I'm just a pilot. As an independent contractor I have made cargo runs for the government, sure. I won't deny that. The money is usually good. Whatever else you seem to think of me, you're way off base."

"Very well, Mister Star," Adler said. "Let's say I believe you."

"You should. It's the truth."

"Be that as it may," Major Adler said, but stopped. He changed direction. "Very well. I will tell you what I am doing here. I think you will be impressed. Follow me."

Lance stood, stretched, and followed his host down the wooden steps to the soft sand and a path that led directly to the camouflage netting. They were almost under the cover of the net when Lance heard a familiar sound. He craned his neck and scanned the skyline.

Major Adler ushered him into the shadows just as the cargo plane came into view at high altitude.

Lance smiled. At least he knew that Buck had gotten the plane up and running. That meant they had a way to get the expedition off the island. He wasn't sure what yet, but something big was about to happen on this island, something quite possibly bigger than a volcanic eruption. That only confirmed his suspicions.

They needed to get off the island.

And they needed to do it soon.

Buck Tellonger maneuvered the plane in for a landing.

The area that Jim Nolan had marked off for use as a landing zone near the camp was a tight fit, but a pilot of Buck's skill had no problem hitting the target. The landing was far smoother than their first landing on this island and the air ace taxied the cargo plane as close to the camp as he could.

Jim Nolan and Nicole Farrington made their way across the knee high grass and met Buck and Red at the cargo door.

"Well?" Jim asked.

"I'm not sure. The Nazis have converted a cove at the southern tip of the island into a base. Nothing too elaborate, but they do have planes and a couple of small buildings."

"And whatever they've got under that camouflage," Red added.

"Any sign of Lance or Cy?" Jim asked.

"We're not sure," Red said. "I thought I saw him, but the people moved under the camouflage so I couldn't be sure."

"So what's the plan, Buck?"

"Right now the plan is the same as it's always been, Jim," Buck said. "We get these folks briefed on the evacuation plan. Then we go pick up our pilots and get the hell out of here."

"I'm all for that," Jim said. "But I don't think Thornby is going to go willingly."

"Did he not feel the earthquake?" Buck asked.

"Jim's right," Nicole said. "The professor is a very stubborn man. It's one of the idiosyncrasies that comes with his position, I'm afraid."

"Yeah, well you just leave him to me," Buck said. "I've been told I can be a little stubborn myself."

"A little..." Red said as he and Jim laughed.

"I'm guessing more than a little," Nicole said.

"You could say that," Jim told her.

"Har. Har. You two are hilarious," Buck said. "Our first priority is dropping whatever unnecessary weight we can from the plane to accommodate the extra passengers."

"On it."

"And while you two take care of that I'll go talk to the professor."

"I'm sorry. You're doing what?"

In his travels, Lance Star had witnessed many an amazing sight. He'd been to the top of the world and even ventured deep beneath the Earth's surface, but never had he heard something that sounded so ridiculous to his ears. His outburst only further served to underscore the ludicrousness of Major Adler's plan.

"Come now, Mister Star," Major Wilhelm Adler said as if addressing a dim-witted child. "Surely, even you can see the brilliance of this operation."

"Brilliance isn't the word I'd use," Lance said. "Crazy is more like it."

They were standing under the camouflaged netting at the Nazi's temporary base. Beneath the netting was another building. This one was far more sanitary than the others, almost antiseptic like a hospital. It was even more so on the inside. Adler referred to it as *The Lab.*

"Crazy?" The major *tsked.* "I am surprised at your shortsightedness, Mister Star. The world as we know it is in a constant state of flux. Even now the strongest nations of the Earth are reaching out their hands across the globe. Once peaceful neighbors have picked up arms in their futile attempt to stave off the inevitable. A full world war will happen, Mister Star. Even you must see that."

"What I see is a bunch of power hungry zealots trying to take what doesn't belong to them," Lance said pointedly. "What I see are small men who act little spoiled children who want the toys the other kids have. You guys talk and talk about uniting the world under one voice, but let's be real, Major, you're nothing but a bunch of bullies picking on the weaker kids."

Lance expected his tirade to result in an unpleasant response, but the major simply smiled and let him say his peace.

"I admire your bravery, Mister Star," Adler said. "There are not many men who would speak to me the way you just did, especially not in the situation such as the one you find yourself."

"My Mom always told me that honesty was the best policy and my Dad used to tell me that shooting my mouth off would land me in trouble. I guess they were both right, huh?"

"Perhaps. Fortunately for you, I am not as quick to order an execution as many of my peers."

"Must be my lucky day," Lance joked.

"Perhaps," Adler said as he walked closer to the window that overlooked the giant cages just off the lab. "I am honestly interested in your thoughts on our plan for these magnificent creatures."

Lance walked up next to the major. From the window he could see the cages holding several pterodactyls. He watched as scientists attached metallic plates to the side of two of the creature's heads, obviously in conjunction with the experiment Adler had told him about. One to a cage, he counted five of them. The other cages were empty, except for the last one where Lance caught sight of Cy Hawkins sitting. At least he knew that his friend was okay and uninjured, as Major Adler had promised.

"I can't explain how these things managed to survive the extinction of their race or how they've managed to stay hidden on this island all these centuries, but they're dinosaurs. Every class I ever took that talked about the history of the dinosaurs contained one similar truth. Despite their enormous size, those things down there have brains about the size of a walnut. They're creatures of instinct, not intelligence."

"An interesting observation."

"What you're proposing is science fiction, Major!" Lance blasted. "They cannot be trained and you're crazy if you think otherwise!"

"Of course they can't," Adler agreed. "Nor would I even try. Trying to teach these beats would be an act of futility and the Reich does not waste tie on futile imperatives. That is the beauty of this plan. Our scientists have developed cutting edge technology that will allow us to control the brain of lesser beings. Using electro-shock impulses, we can give simple commands that even these simple beats can understand. No training required. Just simple obedience."

"You can't be serious."

"Oh, I am very serious. The Wehrmacht's orders are quite specific."

"Oh, well if the Wehrmacht says it's okay, then..." Lance let his voice trail off.

"I see you will need convincing."

"You can say that again, buster."

Major Adler smiled. "Then you are in luck, Mister Star. We have already implanted devices into the brain of two of the creatures. As you can see below, my men are finishing up their work."

Lance watched as the scientists screwed the metal plates into place with large metal bolts. The creatures screeched in pain with each turn of the wrench.

"We were planning to test the subjects today with stationary targets, but your arrival has given me a better option. Since you seem to think that we cannot possibly succeed, I think that you and your associate will make perfect guinea pigs for this test."

"Oh, I don't think so," Lance said.

Adler's friendly demeanor vanished, replaced by the cold hard determination he'd come to expect from a Nazi officer. "I'm sorry, Mister Star. You seem to be under the impression that I am asking for volunteers. I assure you, that is not the case."

"That's good. I hate to volunteer for anything," Lance said, trying to cover the knot forming in the pit of his stomach.

⊕

Lance Star and Cy Hawkins stood in an open field.

They had been escorted to the upper ridgeline under armed guard. Although getting down the incline had been difficult, the Nazis had found a much easier path on the far side of the cove. It was a short hike, but eventually they made it to the clearing.

The grass was easily at knee height and seemed to move in waves in the breeze that swept across the plain. There were a few scattered boulders and rocky outcroppings dotting the landscape and several scattered trees, some of which were quite thick and tall. Lance assumed from their size that they had been there for some time. The molten fury that bubbled below them had been corked up for a long time, possibly even centuries, but he wasn't sure it would be for much longer. The occasional rumble vibrated through the ground. It wasn't as bad as the quake they had felt earlier, but it was enough to concern Lance. Professor Thornby had told him that it was impossible to accurately detect an imminent eruption, but Lance's intuition told him that this particular volcano was only days, maybe even hours, from blowing its top.

The guards left them in the clearing and moved away. Lance assumed they were heading back to the safety of the lab.

"You got a plan?" Cy asked as they each scanned the sky.

"Nothing comes to mind," Lance replied. He had already filled Cy in on Adler's plan and what was about to happen. "Just don't let them catch you."

"That part I already knew."

"If we could get to one of their planes we might have a shot," Lance offered.

"Not a bad idea, but the planes are way down there and we're way up here. I don't think those things are going to give us time to climb down that cliff again," Cy said. "Speaking of…" He pointed.

"I see them," Lance said.

Two of the creatures rose up out of the cove, soaring high into the heavens. Their wing span was incredible, easily matching the size of a small airplane. On the ground, they had looked monstrous, but in flight they were graceful, almost beautiful. They screeched in unison as they soared in an arch, each one staying in perfect formation with the other.

Then they started toward Lance and Cy's direction and started their decent.

"Run!" Lance shouted.

The pilots bolted toward the nearest copse of trees, hoping to lose themselves in the leaves and to stay out of reach of the beast's massive clawed talons. The pterodactyls screamed at their prey as they swooped down with talons extended.

Lance and Cy dove for cover, just seconds ahead of their attackers.

Unable to follow, the giant beasts looped skyward and came around for another pass.

"Well, this is fun," Cy commented as he huddled next to a tree.

"I'm open to suggestions," Lance offered.

Cy thought a moment, then shrugged. "I've got nothing."

"Don't feel bad," Lance said. "Neither do I."

Buck Tellonger had convinced everyone to leave the base camp.

Everyone, that was, except Professor Thornby, who was stubbornly refusing to budge from his monitoring equipment despite Buck's constant haranguing. The constant rumble coming from beneath the ground had helped to convince the others that it was indeed time to go. Convincing the good professor that it was time to go was proving to be a lot less easy. Buck had sent the others ahead to the cargo plane where Red Davis and Jim Nolan were getting them strapped in. The cargo plane was not generally used for ferrying passengers. At best there were two benches that ran across the length of the cargo hold on both sides. There were seatbelts there and also netting that was reserved for strapping down cargo, but could be used in a pinch to strap down passengers.

It wasn't pretty, but it would get them off the island before the volcano erupted. From the almost constant vibration beneath his feet, Buck guessed that the eruption was happening any minute now. In fact, the quakes probably meant it had already started, but hadn't broken through the crust.

Buck was quickly reaching his boiling point with the good professor. Even though Thornby was the client since it was his people who had hired them to deliver Professor Farrington and his equipment, Buck knew that he would have to make a command decision soon. He could either leave Thornby alone on the island, which was a death sentence, or he could forcibly remove the man.

Neither was very palatable, but Buck knew which would help him sleep better at night. He decided to give the professor one more shot at leaving of his own accord before cracking him upside his thick skull. For his own good, of course.

"The pterodactyls ....swooped down with talons extended."

"All right, Professor," Buck said as he burst back into the main tent after getting the last of the scientists heading toward the plane. "We've got everyone on board. All that's left is just you and me so let's get a move on."

"I already told you, Mister Tellonger, my work here is too important to abandon." He was working at a machine that looked like something out of a science fiction pulp novel. Tiny arms left lines of ink on a roll of paper. Small spikes leapt from the steady line in concert with the rumbling beneath their feet.

Buck grabbed the man's arm and spun him around so they stood face to face. "And I told you that we have to get out of here!"

"My work is here!"

"Fine," Buck said and released the man. "Just answer me this one question before I go, Professor. Then I'm out of here."

Thornby turned to face him and placed his hands on his hips in defiance. "Fine. Ask your question."

"When you die on this island, and it is not a question of if, but when," Buck said pointedly. "When you die here who is going to benefit from this precious knowledge you've collected when it dies here with you?"

That brought Thornby up short.

"This is the last train off the island, Professor. Once we're off the ground the only stop we're making is to pick up my friends, then we're going to put as much distance between us and this powder keg we're standing on as possible."

Thornby said nothing.

"Your call," Buck said. "Stay or go."

The professor stared ahead in silence.

"Last chance."

Thornby sighed and seemed to deflate as he made his decision. "You win. We may leave."

"Great. Grab only what you can carry and let's move," Buck said. "I don't think we have much time left."

Suddenly, another quake hit, this one much more powerful than any that had come before it. The ground beneath them bucked wildly, knocking them off balance and throwing both men to the ground.

"Scratch that," Buck said as he helped the professor to his feet. "We are out of time."

"I think you're right," Thornby agreed.

✠

Lance Star had never wished to be in the air more than at that moment.

The ground around him bucked and heaved as the thunderous rumble increased beneath his boot heels. It sounded as though a locomotive was barreling past at top speed and felt comparable to the worst turbulence he'd ever encountered. A couple of trees toppled over near where he and Cy Hawkins crouched, the roots ripping free of the soil that had birthed them.

"This is ridiculous!" Cy shouted.

The shaking started to subside and that's when Lance saw an opening.

"Let's go!" he told Cy and broke from cover and made a beeline for the cove.

The ground quake had knocked the soldiers off balance as much as it had them. The only ones unaffected were the pterodactyls since they were in the air at the time, but since they were fully under the command of their Nazi masters, they didn't give chase. That gave the Sky Rangers a brief window of opportunity.

The soldiers regained their composure about the same time as the pilots neared the edge of the embankment wall. They opened fire on the pilots, but neither Lance nor Cy broke stride as bullets ripped up the ground around their feet.

The pilots reached the edge and instead of stopping, or even slowing, they leapt over the edge and disappeared from view.

Lance and his wingman hit the loose dirt and slid down the embankment. It wasn't the most pleasant of rides, but they reached the bottom quickly, and more importantly, in one piece. Thankfully, they weren't trying to reach the bottom unobserved this time around. The blind spot was too rough to try this maneuver. This time they were more interested in speed than stealth.

At the bottom, both men rolled and came up into a run. They knew that the soldiers would be at the edge soon and start taking potshots at them. Or worse, the big beasts that were after them would catch up.

"Head for the planes!" Lance shouted just ahead of the first shot.

As predicted, the Nazi soldiers opened fore with their rifles. None of the shots hit their mark, although a few did come close. With the never ending rumble vibrating throughout the island, Lance doubted that even the best sharpshooter would have much like lining up a good shot. That worked to his and Cy's advantage.

The pilots each picked out one of the German planes and pulled the chokes from beneath the wheels before heading up the side toward the cockpit. The cockpit canopy was unlocked so Lance slid his backward and dropped into the pilot's seat. It was a two-seater, but could easily be flown by a single pilot.

He looked off to his left just in time to see Cy slide his cockpit canopy closed.

Lance mimicked the maneuver, thumbed the ignition, and let out a yelp of victory when the engine fired.

Major Adler had kept his pilots in a state of constant readiness, which meant that all six of the German planes were kept fully fueled and ready for immediate takeoff. It was a sensible precaution considering the unpredictable nature of the volcano they stood upon. They wouldn't have enough fuel to make it all the way back to the United States, but there were plenty of other islands where they could land and meet up with Buck and the cargo plane. At worse, they could ditch the planes in the ocean, but he would much rather make a present of them to General Walter Pettigrew of the Army Air Corp. Lance suspected that his "Uncle Walter" would enjoy studying these trophies.

Lance pulled the throat mic from his pocket and plugged it into the plane's console. "You there?" he called out once it was in place.

"I'm here, boss," Cy's drawl came back over the speaker. His plane was already starting to roll out of position toward the makeshift runway. Lance nudged his stolen aircraft forward and fell into position behind him. Bullets smacked the ground around the planes, a few even hitting their mark, but those few bounced harmlessly off of the plane's hull.

"I'm on your six," he said. "Let's get moving before these guys get to their planes."

"Roger that. I've got the ball."

Cy's plane took off down the runway like a shot from a cannon. He was only a few feet from the water's edge when the nose lifted and he took to the air. Lance had already started his run before Cy's wheels had left the packed earth. He was only seconds behind Cy as they arced around to get a look at the island.

Lance squeezed his mic. "Buck, are you there?"

"Where the hell have you been?" a familiar gruff voice answered.

Lance let loose a laugh. Despite the life or death situation happening all around him, he found himself smiling the moment he was in the cockpit. He was never as relaxed as when holding the reins of an airplane. Even if it wasn't one of his.

"Stopped off to have a burger and a beer with the new neighbors," Lance said. "We had to leave in a hurry though so Cy and I borrowed a couple of their cars."

"So I take it the two bogeys I've got incoming are you and Cy?" Buck said.

"You got it," Lance said and jiggled the yoke back and forth, which made the plane wiggle in the air. On his wing, he saw Cy copy the maneuver.

"Guess I'll tell Red to hold his fire then," Buck joked.

"That would be appreciated," Lance confirmed. "I wouldn't be surprised if we have company right behind us though."

"I'd say that's a certainty," Buck said as he pointed toward the cove where six new dots rose into the sky. "How many birds did the neighbors have?"

"Six."

"That's what I thought," Buck said. "But I'm counting six bogeys heading your way."

"Two of those are biologics," Lance said.

"I beg your pardon?"

"You heard me," Lance said. "The Nazis have been experimenting on those big birds you were worried about. They've got control helmets on those two."

"You're joking?"

"Sadly, no," Lance added.

"How did they--"

"No time for that now, Buck," Lance said. "We need to get off this rock A.S.A.P. Or sooner. Thornby's group?"

"All present and accounted for," Buck said. "We're ready to blow this joint anytime you are. Just say the word."

"Consider it said," Lance added. "Head for open water. Cy and I will cover your six."

"Roger that."

"Cy, you with me?"

"Loud and clear, boss."

"You ready to go to work?"

"More than ready."

"Then let's do this," Lance said as he changed direction.

☩

There were few pilots as skilled in air combat as those of the Luftwaffe. The Wehrmacht pilots were formidable combatants in the air and were known to rain down death from above. Lance Star had encountered more than one run in with the likes of them in recent years. So, yes, they were skilled flyers, but they couldn't touch the Sky Rangers when it came to piloting prowess.

"Maneuver Beta Blue," Lance called into the throat mic.

"Roger, Beta Blue," Cy called back.

"Break and roll on my mark."

A beat passed.

"Mark!"

Cy dove right as Lance broke left. The incoming Nazi planes split their formation, two after the first target and two after the second, exactly as the Sky Rangers had intended. Beta Blue was a maneuver they had used before, but it generally worked. Breaking formation was generally seen as an act of desperation. It is constantly drilled into pilots during training that they are never, ever, to leave their wingman's side in a fight. Breaking formation gave the enemy the upper hand.

All of this was true, but the Sky Rangers had created a maneuver that used this to their advantage. And it almost always worked.

Lance noticed that the prehistoric troops were hanging back. He assumed that Major Adler was still on the ground, controlling them from their base. Suddenly, he wondered what kind of range the beast's control helmets had on them. As much as he wanted to know, he would have to put aside his curiosity for a moment. He would worry about the beasts when the time came.

The lead Luftwaffe plane opened up with its machine guns and Lance took his borrowed plane into a steep barrel roll. It was a maneuver he had performed many times, but usually in a plane he was familiar with. Thankfully, the German planes were well made. They were built to perform.

Lance toggled his guns to hot as the ground rushed up to meet him. Then, when it looked like he was headed for a big crash, Lance pulled the plane into an arc and soared back into the sky, opening up with all of his guns at once.

But not at the plane that was after him.

Cy Hawkins had performed a similar dive and arc with his plane. The trajectory of the Beta Blue scenario brought Cy out of his arc with a clear shot of the plane chasing Lance. Conversely, Lance now had a perfect bead on the plane that had been in pursuit of his wingman.

The Nazi plane was hit broadside as a steady stream of bullets tore through the plane's canopy, killing the pilot instantly. Without a pilot to control her, the plane angled toward the deck and plowed into the ground at full speed, exploding on impact. Half a second later, the plane Cy shot down followed suit.

And, as if on cue, the island responded in kind.

"Make for open water!" Lance shouted into his mic. "This thing's about to blow."

Thick geysers of dark gray ash shot into the sky with enough force that the nearby planes were nearly rattled part from the concussive waves of force radiating outward from the island. One of the Nazi pilots pursuing Cy's plane wasn't able to react quickly enough and was caught in the blast of ash. Knocked off course, the plane tumbled out of control end over end until it slammed into the broken ground below and exploded

"That just leaves Adler," Lance said as she watched the plane engulfed in flame below him.

"And his pets," Cy's voice shouted across the wireless speaker. "Incoming!"

Lance spun just in time to see the mass of scaled flesh barreling toward him. The creature was fast and it led with its talons open. Its claws were easily six inches long, each one razor sharp and able to rip a man in half with little difficulty.

Before the air ace could react, the pterodactyl slammed into the side of the plane with all of the force and speed of a locomotive. The thick glass shell of the canopy spider-webbed as cracks arced across the surface like tiny lightning bolts. The plane immediately went off course as the cockpit instruments started spinning out of control. Sparks poured from busted panels and the acrid smell of smoke filled Lance's nostrils.

The plane dropped like a stone, but the prehistoric monster refused to let go as its talons tore into the glass and metal surrounding the pilot's head. He could hear Cy shouting his name, but Lance wasn't able to respond. His borrowed plane was dead. He released the seatbelt latch and moved away from the talons as they pressed the plating in on him.

There was no chance of ejecting because he couldn't slide the cockpit aside with the extra weight atop it. And even if he did get it open he wasn't wearing a parachute, but that was a problem he didn't have to deal with until he got free of the cockpit. He'd always suspected that he would die in a cockpit. He just didn't want it to be this one. And he wasn't ready to go now.

Lance pulled his gun and aimed for the creature's underbelly, hoping that it was an easier area to penetrate as with so many other animals. If he could make the blasted beast relax its grip he might be able to bail out. Then he would have to worry about that lack of a parachute problem.

Lance fired until the clip was empty.

The pterodactyl screamed in pain and rage, rattling the wounded plane in its grip like stubborn prey that refused to die.

Lance slapped a new clip into place and opened fire until it was also empty. He was about to repeat the process with his last clip when the beast let go of the plane and sailed off. He could only see it for a brief moment, but it had appeared to be spiraling downward toward the deck. He must have hurt it.

There was no time to revel in his victory, however. Although the monster was no longer tearing the plane apart, it was still falling, and this time there was nothing fighting against gravity. With little time to spare, Lance braced himself and kicked open the cockpit frame. It opened, but the bent metal stopped it from sliding completely open. It was enough for him to squeeze through however and Lance pushed himself through the opening.

Just as a hail of bullets smacked into the side of the plane.

Major Adler's plane strafed the plane and smoke poured from the dead plane's engine. Lance knew he was a sitting duck. With nothing to lose he unloaded the last clip from his pistol firing at the major's plane. It was a last ditch effort, but ultimately a futile one. He was too far away to do any real damage.

Cy Hawkins, on the other hand, was a real challenge.

Cy's plane came at Adler's plane from the side, pouring fire directly into the plane, which erupted into flames and trailed thick black plumes of smoke behind it.

Lance watched the major's plane drop and disappear into the gray ash that had almost completely covered the island below. He pushed himself through the open cockpit and signaled Cy, who gave him a big thumbs up before lifting the nose of his plane and falling back.

Lance closed his eyes, said a silent prayer.

And jumped.

⌗

Cy Hawkins had been flying from the time he was tall enough to reach the rudder pedals. Coming from a farming community where crop-dusting was a way of life, he discovered a love and affinity for flying. Then he went to war and learned some very hard lessons about the power he controlled from inside the cockpit. But it wasn't until he hooked up with Lance and the Sky Rangers that he learned what it truly meant to be a pilot, to be an air ace. He'd done more in the pilot's seat of a plane in the last few years than most men ever dreamed of doing. He'd seen and done so much that he thought there were no more firsts for him as a pilot.

He was wrong.

Lance's plan was simple.

Crazy, but simple.

Cy watched as Lance leapt from his dropping plane. He positioned his arms and legs to keep him aloft and slow his descent, as if he were parachuting. The only difference was that Lance was not wearing a parachute.

Cy dropped the German plane into position and slowed his acceleration to come in below Lance. It was tricky flying under the best of circumstances, but he was about to add an additional challenge. He popped the canopy and slid it open. Instantly, wind and ash whipped past him, stinging his exposed skin. The smell of sulfur filled the air and the roar of the eruption happening nearby was almost deafening.

He put all of that out of his mind. The only thing he had to concentrate on was catching Lance. If they missed the mark there wasn't time to make a second attempt.

"Come on, come on, come on…" Cy muttered.

Lance angled toward Cy's position.

Although this wasn't the first time he'd jumped out of a plane, it wasn't even his first time doing so sans parachute, but it was the first time he did so with the intention of landing in another. It was a tricky move that he would never have considered under normal circumstances, but with nothing left to lose, it had seemed like his only option at the time.

The volcano continued to belch toxic smoke into the sky and visibility was all but gone. Lance knew there was only one shot at getting this right.

Cy's plane came up fast and he slammed into it a bit harder than anticipated. Lance grabbed at the open cockpit and managed to hold on. Cy's hand them grabbed hold and pulled him inch by inch until he was inside the cockpit.

Cy slid the canopy closed and let out the breath he had been holding.

Both men coughed.

"You okay?" Cy asked.

"I'll tell you in a minute," Lance said as he righted himself in the co-pilot's seat. "Let's put some distance between us and this island first, what do you say?"

"You got it, boss."

Minutes later, they settled into position next to the cargo plane and Lance radioed Buck on the Sky Rangers' private frequency.

"What kept you?" Buck growled in response.

"Took the scenic route," Lance joked.

"You're a laugh riot, Lance. Do you know how close you cut it back there?"

"If he doesn't, I do" Cy cut in.

"Let's go home, boys," Lance said.

The Sky Rangers set a course for home as the island volcano exploded behind them.

THE END.

HERE WE GO AGAIN. FLYING INTO THE UNKNOWN.

No sooner had **Lance Star: Sky Ranger Volume 3** gone into production than plans started coming together for the book that you hold in your hand. Lance and the Sky Rangers are special characters to me and I've grown quite fond of each and every one of them. Even the villains, but we'll get back to them in a minute.

I've written several Lance Star tales by this point, including three novellas for the prose line, several comic book adventures, and work progresses on a Lance Star novel that will feature a big knock down drag out battle between Lance and Baron Otto Von Blood. There's another of those good bad guys. When writing a character I've written numerous times before I often ask myself what I can do to make this one stand out from the others I've written.

My Lance Star: Sky Ranger stories to date have all been fairly well set in the real world. This was a decision I made early on. I liked seeing Lance and the team dealing with very real and plausible situations. Some of the other writers have penned more fantastical tales and those are always fun to read. For Volume 4 I decided it was time to let the sci-fi writer in me have a crack at the Sky Rangers. I had already established that most of the characters I write live in the same world. It's a little fun thing I like to do. Since that means characters like Secret Agent X can meet Lance, and I've had X fight a monster (look for **Secret Agent X Volume 4** from Airship 27) then it stood to reason that Lance could too.

The idea of a mysterious island is certainly not a new one. There have been movies, books, and TV series based on that simple conceit, but it seemed like a very pulpy place for the Sky Rangers to visit. Throwing Nazis, an annoying academic, and a volcano ready to erupt into the mix ratcheted up the suspense. The story originally featured pirates as well, but the story went long and I had to cut them to get the word count down to where it needed to be.

The idea of the Sky Rangers planes being attacked by pterodactyls was a visual I couldn't get out of my head so I made sure that happened in the story. Imagine my surprise when it became the cover to this very collection you hold in your hands.

And then there was the villain.

Major Wilhem Adler started out as just another Nazi officer, but as I got to know the character he became more and more interesting. Could that be why his demise in the story is not focused on too grandly? Could we see him again? Hmmm... Could be. You know you can't keep a good villain down.

I'd like to thank the writers and artists involved with this volume for the care and attention they've focused on Lance and the Sky Rangers. As always, where would we be without the tireless efforts of Airship 27's Ron Fortier and Rob Davis, who help get these books out of the hangar and into the hands of readers like yourself?

Well, that's enough rambling from me. Thank you for picking up **Lance Star: Sky Ranger Volume 4**. Looking forward to seeing you for Volume 5 and in the upcoming novel, "Cold Snap", whichever comes first.

And don't forget to stop by www.lance-star for news, interviews, and all things Lance Star. We'd love to hear from you so please leave us a comment or two.

Ready on the flight line.

BOBBY NASH - From his secret lair in the wilds of Bethlehem, Georgia, 2013 Pulp Ark Award Winning Best Author, Bobby Nash writes a little bit of everything including novels, comic books, short prose, graphic novels, screenplays, media tie-ins, and more.

Between writing deadlines, Bobby is an actor and extra in movies and television, including appearances in Deviant Pictures' *Fat Chance*, FOX's *The Following*, USA's *Neil, Inc.*, AMC's *Halt and Catch Fire*, and more. He is also the co-host of the Earth Station One podcast (www.esopodcast.com) and a member of the International Association of Media Tie-in Writers.

Bobby was named Best Author in the 2013 Pulp Ark Awards, his first professional writing award. Rick Ruby, from Airship 27's **The Ruby Files** series, a character co-created by Bobby and author Sean Taylor also snagged a Pulp Ark Award for Best New Pulp Character of 2013. Bobby has also been nominated for the 2014 New Pulp Awards and Pulp Factory Awards for his work.

Ring of Fire marks Bobby's 7th completed Lance Star: Sky Ranger story. His work has appeared in all four Lance Star: Sky Ranger anthologies as well as the Lance Star *"One Shot!"* comic book. Two more comic stories are completed and coming soon. The Lance Star novel, *"Cold Snap"* is also coming along, ironically at a glacial pace, though Bobby swears he'll get back to it soon.

For more information on Bobby Nash please visit him at:
www.bobbynash.com,
www.facebook.com/AuthorBobbyNash,
and www.twitter.com/bobbynash, among other places across the web.

Lance Star

"The Devil's Arm Gambit"

by
Andrew Salmon

There was nothing about the flight that hinted at impending disaster. The airplane had glided smoothly into a morning sky as blue as a robin's egg. Only the barest hint of a breeze promising the baking heat to come in the Nevada desert caressed the gleaming silver aircraft as it ascended. Bright, clear sunlight struck the gleaming metal hull, exploding into a million diamonds.

The eight passengers settled into their seats, lighting cigarettes, adjusting pillows or gazing absently out at the nearby mountain ranges permanently topped with traces of snow the heat of the surrounding desert couldn't reach. Some of the passengers opened their windows for a better view or to make an attempt at a photograph. Low conversation and the snap of an early afternoon newspaper being straightened were the only sounds above the drone of the engines. For thirty minutes the miracle of air travel lulled the passengers on this perfect, cloudless afternoon.

A stewardess offered sandwiches when the lunch hour was upon them. Wax paper crinkled. Coffee in china cups was dispensed.

Then the ship bucked.

This startled the passengers but they thought nothing of it. The desert winds could be tricky and such turbulent conditions were the norm during air travel.

The plane heaved and the passengers were tossed out of their seats. Cups crashed, men and women sprawled as the plane pitched nose down in a lethal dive.

While shrieks and yells sounded throughout the cabin and minds raced with thoughts of death, the plane gradually levelled out. The engines beat a steady tempo and the passengers slowly rose to their feet, eyes wide and shining as they resumed their seats.

The stewardess, clearly rattled but putting on a brave face, straightened her cap and made her way to the cockpit on unsteady pins.

She was met at the threshold by the pilot, Jethro Garcia. This was not her first flight with Garcia, she knew the man well as he was dating a friend of hers. Her professional demeanor slipped while her back was to the passengers and the terror she had experienced moments before showed on her pretty face.

Garcia, tall and lean, was unruffled and she drew strength from his relaxed air. He filled the doorway but she could see the back of Dennis

Buck, the co-pilot, slumped in his seat but gazing straight ahead out the window.

Garcia returned her strained smile.

"That was a little rough, Jet," she said, forcing levity into her tone. "What …?"

Jet Garcia whipped up the bayonet he had concealed behind his leg and plunged it into the stomach of the stewardess. Guiding it upwards as it pierced her flesh, the knife sliced into her heart and she crumpled to the floor with a soft gasp.

A few of the passengers saw the woman spasm as she collapsed. However before they could investigate or even cry out, Garcia stepped over the dead stewardess and stood before the perplexed and horrified passengers.

He gripped the bayonet in one hand and a black .45 in the other.

"Change of plans, ladies and gentlemen," he announced. He gave them a good look at the gun. "Get 'em up!"

At first the men and women stared dumbly at Garcia but the weapons spoke volumes. The cold eyes of the man holding the gun did not rest. Pairs of hands rose to the roof of the cabin.

"Go ahead and rob us, partner," a big Texan in an ox-blood suit said, jovially, "You ain't making a getaway up here."

Garcia shot the man in the stomach. A woman screamed as the Texan bellowed and collapsed into his seat.

"Anyone else got observations?" Garcia asked. Had the stewardess been amongst the living, she might have been struck by the strange voice coming from Garcia's lips. But for the passengers, the levelled gun and the groans of the gravely wounded Texan was all they cared about.

"Leave him!" Garcia spat to a couple that bent to aid the sprawled and bleeding man. He grabbed an empty mail sack and tossed it into the aisle. "Place your valuables in that!"

The passengers stared at him mutely. The Texan moaned.

"Move!" Garcia shouted. He thrust the gun forward.

The cabin erupted into activity. Rings, watches, wallets and necklaces were thrust into the bag by desperate hands. The bag soon bulged to Garcia's satisfaction. He instructed one of the women to bring it to him. Grabbing it out of her outstretched hand, he tucked the top of the mail bag through his belt loop.

"All right, you lot!" he instructed. "Move to the back of this ship."

During the commotion at the bag, Garcia had yanked a parachute from beneath an empty seat in the first row. He was just finishing buckling it on when he gave the order to move. He checked the straps a second time with one hand, the other clutching the automatic which never wavered.

"Here's what happens now," he began as he stepped lithely to the cabin door. "I'm going out for a little sky walk and Heaven help any one of you who moves before I'm gone. Got that?" He jerked a thumb over his shoulder. "The co-pilot back there will fly you in after I'm gone."

Garcia glanced at his watch, then proceeded to open the door. A windstorm erupted in the cabin. Anything not bolted down swirled in the vortex. Some of the female passengers screamed above the shrieking wind. The men clutched at their hats saucering around the narrow space.

Garcia gave the passengers a mock salute. His lips parted in a hideous grin as he dove through the open door.

The passengers closest to the port side pressed their noses against the glass, saw a parachute billow stark white against the brown earth below.

Three of the men rushed up the aisle to the cockpit. They bellowed at the co-pilot who did not turn around. One man, a doctor, bent over the corpse of the stewardess, another stepped over the sprawled woman. The third lost his footing in the pool of blood coating the floor of the cockpit. The first man strode to the co-pilot. "Get on the radio to the police! Hurry!"

The co-pilot did not even flinch.

The passenger gripped the man's shoulder and the co-pilot toppled to one side. His throat had been gashed from ear to ear.

There was no one flying the plane.

A sudden explosion beneath the pilot's panel shattered the grisly silence. The plane nosed down, the clear blue sky through the windows was replaced by the jagged peaks of mountains looming before them. Everyone was thrown to the floor as the plan plummeted.

The man nearest the explosion ignored the shrapnel in his legs and lunged for the pilot stick. The lever jounced freely in his fist. The explosion had severed the control stick and destroyed the piloting controls.

"Oh, no," was all the man said.

Screams and shouts resounded in the plane as it rocketed down out of control. It exploded in a yellow-orange fireball when it struck the rocky cliffs near one of the highest ranges in Nevada. Debris and body parts poured down the side of the mountain as a cloud of thick black smoke billowed into the clear sky.

Jet Garcia landed smoothly, rolling to absorb the impact. He got out of the chute and gathered it into his arms. He was only a mile from an access road and saw the trail of dust from the approaching automobile.

He'd come down close to a narrow ravine. A sliver of stream snaked through some one hundred feet below in the dark cool shadows between the pressing rock walls. Garcia pulled the mail sack free of his belt and set it down at his feet. Then he reached up and pulled at his face. Jet Garcia's features became so much torn latex rubber as the thief pulled the mask from his true face.

He wadded up the rubber and jammed it into the mail sack. Leaning over the crevice between the rock walls of the ravine, he tossed the bulging sack down into the crack and turned to await his ride back. The top of the sack had not been fastened and a cascade of gold jewellery and currency spewed from the bag as it fell to the water below.

The car pulled up, slewing in the loose sand and scrub brush. The man who had been Jet Garcia stepped into the car.

"Well?" the driver asked.

"Went off without a hitch," the thief replied now speaking with a slight German accent.

The driver threw the car into gear and they drove off.

Lance Star dropped the Skybolt II down three hundred feet and banked right. Etched in the chalky brown earth below were the straight borders of a runway.

"When was the last time you saw Herbert Smith?" Lance asked his wingman over the radio.

"Just after the war," Buck Tellonger replied. "After he made Squadron Leader. They reassigned him and we lost touch until I ran across him stateside five years ago."

They could see the airfield below. Metal huts glinted in the sun with roads leading off to the nearby town. Planes dotted the field, looking like great white crosses. Men moved about the field.

"I take it you don't believe what the papers are saying?" Lance asked.

"Ah, that's a lot of hooey!" Buck replied. "Smitty is as straight as the day is long. I'd stake my reputation on that!"

"Well, something is out of joint and we've got to get to the bottom of it," Red Davis said from the Skybolt's other cockpit. "It ain't every day General Pettigrew assigns us to an out of the way airfield."

The plane continued its smooth descent. The wheels cranked down and

Lance Star expertly set the plane down on the runway. He turned the ship to guide it over the main hangar. Buck mirrored Lance's movements with the Hornet he flew. Two autos were already racing out to intercept them and the area around the hangar was crawling with staff milling about.

Lance throttled down and brought the plane to a complete stop a considerable distance from the hangar offices. Buck did likewise with his Hornet. Lance, Buck and Red stepped down to the tarmac. A wave of dry, choking heat hit them like a wall. The cars bracketed the planes, skidding to a halt in clouds of dust. Doors flew open.

"Your buddy has a strange way of making new arrivals feel welcome," Lance observed.

"It is queer."

One of the men climbing out of the car was Herbert Smith. Buck pointed him out. "You can ask him about it yourself. Here he comes."

Smith strode forward to meet them but the serious expression on his cadaverous face didn't change even when he recognized Buck who gave him a brief wave and flashed a smile. The men around Smith fanned out around the plane, keeping their distance.

"Lance Star," Smith said, taking Lance's offered hand in a weak grip that didn't go with the man's athletic build. "I've heard a lot about you. Gotta hope it's true."

Buck came forward and pounded Smith on the shoulder with one hand and pumped his hand with the other. "Believe it, Smitty," he said, concern in his eyes to go with his forced joviality. He had read the worry in his old friend's face. "There's nothing the Sky Rangers can't handle. Whatever you're problems are, we'll fix 'em."

Red provided the same assurances by way of a greeting.

Smith seemed to buck up under the assurances and the creases in his forehead were not so pronounced. "Look, let's get out of this sun and have a tall, cold one."

"Now you're speaking my language," Buck bellowed.

"Not so fast." One of the men stepped forward. He was dressed in workman's overalls but he carried himself with a distinctively military air.

Smith turned to face him. "Relax, these are the men the General sent."

"Say, what is this?" Lance asked.

"I'll explain it all inside," Smitty assured. "Come on. We don't have a lot of time."

╬

Minutes later they were all gathered around a conference table. Fans blew hot air around the room, ice clinked in glasses. The Sky Rangers endured the scrutiny their papers were given by the mysterious man who never left Smith's side. Satisfied, the man had returned the papers, then nodded curtly to Smith.

"Someone is trying to run me out of business and they're doing a hell of a job," Smith began.

"We learned as much from the general," Lance broke in. "We can't help you without the facts. So, let's have them."

"You read about the crash," Smith said. It was not a question. "That was my best plane and my best pilot."

"Tough break, but these things happen," Red said. "Are you telling us there's more to it?"

Smith nodded, dejectedly. "The plane hit high up on the Nevada range and we haven't picked over the whole site yet."

"You've notified the families at least," Lance offered.

"Yeah, from the passenger list. You see we haven't recovered a wallet or pocketbook. Not one. From eight passengers. Not one piece of identification. And we're a body short. Jet Garcia's body is nowhere to be found."

"That's not unusual," Lance explained. "The report said the wreckage spilled down the mountainside. After the plane went in pretty hard, as I understand it."

"I hear what you're saying and that's how we figured it. Until they dug a .45 slug out of one of the dead passengers. Gut shot so the docs say. Not long before the crash."

"Robbery?" Lance concluded.

"So the story goes," Smith agreed. "All of the passengers' valuables are gone, one of them is shot up and Garcia is missing. It's like he never got on that plane."

"Okay," Buck said, his stocky frame tensed. "There's a sky pirate on the loose. We'll bring him in and clear the whole mess up."

"I'm afraid it's not that simple," the man at Smith's elbow spoke up.

Smith leaned forward and placed his elbows on the desk. "The crash. The robbery... Word is getting around and clients are cancelling by the bushel. I'll be out of business in a month."

"It can't be as bad as that," Buck observed.

"You don't understand. There's one client I simply can't afford to lose."

The man in overalls raised both hands, bringing the discussion to a halt. "That's enough for now. We need... "

Another overalled man stepped briskly into the conference room and strode towards the man with his arms out. Whispers were exchanged. They grew emphatic. Nods were exchanged. The man lowered his arms. He then looked over the assembled men, crossed his arms and scrutinized Lance before reluctantly addressing the group.

"All right. Your clearances have been checked and authenticated. It's time we filled you in on things here. My name is Culver. And this... "

Before he could utter another word a slip of a man with a mop of curly blonde hair burst into the room. He was middle-aged yet spry. His crab-like hands, black with oil, opened and closed convulsively. His name was Jim McPhee.

"It's that kraut again, Smitty," McPhee's voice was a deep baritone which offset his emaciated form. "He's just drove in with some of his crew."

"Mr. Zimmer is not authorized to be here," Culver cautioned. "Same goes for his crew. My men and I will explain this to them."

"Nothing doing," Smith countered. "This is my field and my business. I'll handle it."

With that Smith was up like a shot and began steaming towards the door.

"Zimmer pulled up with a handful of his flunkies," the gangly McPhee explained as he moved aside to let his boss through the doorway, then followed behind. "I had the boys keep an eye on them. You should'a seen 'em all stomping around like they owned the place."

"Zimmer tell you what he wanted?"

"I didn't ask. I figured to fetch you so you could run that kraut off."

"That is precisely what I intend to do."

Lance Star, Tellonger and Davis were behind the airmen as this exchange took place. It was clear they would need more information if they were to make heads or tails out of what was going on.

"Who is this Zimmer when he's home?" Lance asked.

"Heinrich Zimmer," Smith spat over his shoulder as they all stepped out into the scorching sun. "Was a killing ace during the war. Now he's trying to run me out of business."

"Are you talking about the Sky Reaper?" Buck asked.

"The same."

Red whistled in astonishment. "That's one tough customer."

"He's a lying, scheming saboteur!"

"Those are serious charges," Lance observed. "Can you prove any of them?"

"Not just now," Smith replied. "But his time is coming, I promise you that. I'll get the goods on him or tear that skunk limb from limb. No odds on which it'll be first. For now though, he's trespassing and we'll just see about that!"

Lance stepped up and then walked shoulder to shoulder with Smith. They spoke in low tones. "Look, your man said Zimmer drove in. How long a drive is it back to his field?"

"Thirty minutes!" Smith blurted. "So what?"

"Can you stall them along here?"

"Why?"

"Flying beats motoring," Lance explained. "My crew and I will fly out to Zimmer's operation and poke around while he's here with his cronies. Might turn up something."

"I don't know…?"

"Smith, if you're certain Zimmer is behind the setbacks you've suffered, then you'll need hard evidence to prove it. We'll be in and out before that bunch can make it back. What do you say?"

"I'd as soon shoot Zimmer as look at him," Smith said, "but I'll try to string 'em along. No promises though. If that nest of vipers cracks wise or tries to strong arm me, then that'll be all she wrote and I'll toss 'em off my property."

"Do the best you can," Lance encouraged.

The blazing sun enveloped them in a shroud of heat as the Sky Rangers splintered off from the group and crossed the open space between the office and the main hangar. Past Smith's shoulder, Lance could see two groups squared off against each other. One, Smith's people, stood abreast of the hangar entrance, wrenches and spanners clutched in their grimy fists. Facing them, with their backs to Smith and the others, stood half a dozen men in identical tan suits. Despite the heat, these men were hatless, their cropped blonde hair burnished by the relentless sun. Belching a cloud of black smoke against the cobalt sky, an aircraft engine droned off to one side. An open tool box lay open on the ground next to it.

"Where are Star and the others going?" Culver asked.

Smith told him.

Culver whipped his head around and gazed after the Sky Rangers. His lips set and he snorted at Smith. "There's more going on here than they know. Loose canons will sink this operation."

Lance spied a DC-3 nearby and they scrabbled aboard. Voices reached them thinly across the arid air. Lance saw Smith and Culver exchange heated words, then the group approached Zimmer and crew.

"What's the big idea?" Smith demanded as he swung around the parked Duesenberg Zimmer and party had arrived in and confronted the former Ace.

Zimmer, the tallest member of the visiting group turned. Heinrich Zimmer was well-proportioned, muscular, his face square and ruggedly handsome. Impeccably dressed, hair even and immaculate; only the man's wiry eyebrows made him appear human rather than something hewn from cold marble.

"Nice of you to join us," Zimmer addressed Smith, his German accent subdued but present. "Decent of you to spare my having to track you down."

"You and your crew are on my property," Smith countered. "State your business or be on your way."

Zimmer chuckled. "You truly believe this is still your operation. After the setbacks you've experienced recently? This is not a going concern. Or is it possible I have not snatched up all of your clients yet? I assure you I will get them all."

"Like hell!"

Lance set the DC-3's engines roaring and drowned out the rest of the conversation. It was bad timing considering what followed, but the plane was already jouncing down the runway by the time the scene took a turn for the worst.

"I am not an unreasonable man," Zimmer went on, smoothly. "I have come to make you an offer on your field. Surely even someone like yourself can see that you are beaten. I offer a fair price, one much higher than is necessary given your recent operational setbacks."

"All right, that's it! Clear out, I say!" Smith's voice took on an icy tone. "That is the last you'll hear from me. My fists will pick up the conversation if you lot don't about face and march!"

Zimmer was unmoved by Smith's threats. However his point had been made and he saw no reason to continue the charade. He shrilled a short whistle and his men fell back to cluster about the Duesenberg. Zimmer turned and addressed Culver. "Let me know when you are ready to deal."

Zimmer joined his men and they climbed inside the machine. The engine purred to life and the car moved off. The tension gradually eased as the car receded.

Then a grumbling airplane engine exploded.

A shock ran through the group at the unexpected noise.

"Damn it, Jim!" Smith roared. "Was that the motor for the T-32?"

"I was working on it when that bunch pulled in," McPhee replied.

"They go anywhere near it?"

"Not that I noticed." He ran to the smoking engine, used a rag to protect his fingers while he shut the thing own. His expert eyes squinted at the charred ruin.

"Anything?" Smith enquired.

The man shook his head hesitantly. "Not that I can see. To be honest, she might have gone on her own. Or those mooks messed with it. I can't tell."

"Damn, Zimmer!" Smith stamped.

"Easy, Smith," Culver soothed. "They want you to lose your head. Besides it may already be too late for you."

Once again in the air, Lance Star wanted more information on the Sky Reaper as he aimed the nose of the plane east towards Zimmer's field. He'd heard of the man of course – a romanticism was springing up around those early days of aviation – but it would take hard facts about the former ace if he was going to prove Zimmer was behind the tragedies Smith's outfit had suffered.

"I never flew against him," Buck admitted. "But I heard the stories. The man was like ice on the stick. You couldn't rattle him."

"I read that he didn't fly very long," Lance offered.

"That's right. Word had it he became a Hun spy, real cloak and dagger stuff. That was courtesy of some captured German airman so happy to be out of the war, they talked a blue streak. Who knows, really? There were a lot of tall tales bandied about during the fighting."

"If it's true that Zimmer was an operative," Lance mused, "he was never caught. If he had been, I doubt he would be allowed to open an air service on American soil. There might be something to it though. Let's stay sharp."

"Lance, how are we going to get down there?" Red asked.

"Yeah," Buck added, "if Zimmer is pulling some sort of monkey business, it's unlikely he'll let us just drop in out of the sky."

"I thought of that," Lance replied as he banked the silver craft. They could see Zimmer's airfield sprawled out across the parched sand beneath them. It was an impressive spread with two low office blocks and three massive hangars. "Get them on the squawk box."

No sooner were the words out of Lance Star's mouth that the plane lost

"She might have gone on her own."

trim and began to wobble. The craft dipped a hundred feet in the process and the men gripped the armrests of their seats as Lance manipulated the stick.

"I know your Daddy taught you to fly better than that!" Tellonger chided.

Lance ignored the comment. "Tell them we've got mechanical difficulties but don't mention my name. As far as they're concerned it's just you two aboard. Got it?"

Buck nodded as the air traffic controller's voice rattled out of the radio. Tollenger identified himself before saying, "We need to bring this ship down. She's fighting us all the way. Can we make an emergency landing?"

"What's the trouble?"

"Damned if I know," roared Buck. And he was telling the truth.

Lance rose up out of the pilot's chair and motioned Red into it.

"Where are you off to?" Red hissed.

Lance smirked. "I'm going aft to break something. Got to make our story convincing."

It took a tense couple of minutes to convince the controller but permission to land was given at last. The time was apropos as the plane began to lose fuel and altitude at an alarming rate; for real this time as Lance had doctored a fuel line.

"Don't make it look too good, Lance!" Buck hollered over his shoulder as he worked the controls. The man was one of the best pilots in the world. Under his deft control, the plane glided in with only the odd bump to sell the feigned distress needed to force a landing. The plane taxied between the massive hangars and jerked to a stop fifty yards from the administration building. A ground crew was waiting to greet them. That greeting was not going to be friendly judging from the scowls on the men's faces. They came forward after Tellonger cut the engines. The looks they shot up at the cockpit indicated to the two Rangers that the safe landing Tellonger had just pulled off did not make their day.

Buck and Red exited the cockpit and headed quickly to the hatch. They wanted to reach it before Zimmer's crew could pile inside, start poking around and tumble to wherever Lance had hidden himself. They got the door open and hopped down to the sandy tarmac just as Zimmer's people reached the plane.

"I can't thank you fellas enough," Red said, good-naturedly as he looked over the group. There were four muscular men, all in identical grey coveralls and all as tall as Red's six-foot-one. "Things were kind of hairy up there."

A steely-eyed man with a face that had absorbed more than its share of hard knocks stepped up quickly. "What's the trouble?"

Red shook his head and pulled at one ear. "No clue. She got lazy on us and we dropped like a stone."

The man put on an act of false camaraderie. "My name is Koller. I am in charge here. We'll find the trouble and have you on your way in nothing flat." He motioned his men towards the plane.

Lance was seconds from discovery and that would be all she wrote. Red acted.

"We appreciate the hospitality, brother," he said. "We really do. But we don't want to put your people at risk. These engines were running pretty damn hot on the way down. What do you say we give these babies a chance to cool some before your crew goes to work? Besides, me and my buddy here had a hairy experience up there. Any chance we can get a belt of something to steady us while we wait for the ship's mood to improve?"

The hard-eyed Koller considered this. He came to a decision and stretched his bloodless lips into a hack artist's rendition of a smile. "You are right, gentlemen," he said, his tones flat, lifeless. "Let's go inside and we'll have a drink."

Lance Star nodded approvingly as his Sky Rangers were guided inside the squat office building near the arcing hangar. They had left the cabin door open as well, which would permit the young aviator to drop to the tarmac quietly and easily.

He peered quickly around one corner of the door. The coast was clear. Moving silent as the wind, he dropped down and lost himself in the cool shadow beneath the plane's underbelly. He squatted next to one of the landing gear and determined if it was safe to move.

The danger of discovery out in the open between the hangar and the office was very real – albeit remote. Bright sunlight lit the entire area. Bordered by the gleaming white walls of the office block and the hangar, the light was reflecting off these surfaces only added to the shimmer. The shadow beneath the plane appeared black as pitch by contrast.

Be that as it may, Lance was aware that the faked engine trouble which had gotten them on the ground was a double-edged sword. Zimmer's men were no doubt anxious about having strangers on the premises without their boss around to call the shots so it seemed likely they would make that drink Red had wrangled a short one before getting the plane back up into the air and away from there as quickly as possible. This, plus the fact that Zimmer was on his way back with more of his goons made their position all the more precarious.

Scanning around for potential prying eyes, Lance was surprised at how few men he saw. A field of this size required a much larger staff than what he was seeing – even knowing ahead of time that five men were en route with Zimmer.

Lance filed this bit of information away and got moving – grateful for the few staff as it allowed him more freedom of movement. With one eye on the office door, Lance glided out from the cover of the landing gear and dashed to the far wall of the block not ten feet from the maw of the hangar. The area was deserted. He sidled to the corner of the building and peeked around. The office block was considerably longer than it was wide and a series of short staircases led to doors. These had to be the quarters of some kind.

He made it to the hangar undetected. As he was about to ease into the cavernous space, he heard low voices. Two men speaking German, which Lance did not understand. Lance took cover behind a rack of parts close to the outer wall and strained his ears. The men stepped out and ambled off to the facing hangar.

Each second was precious, Lance knew, so he swung around and into the now vacant hangar, hugging the wall.

The hangar was deserted. An eerie silence pervaded. Lance had eased gingerly around the entrance in the hopes of a quick glance without being spotted by the field's staff and to ensure that the men were all at work, leaving him free to examine the building across the way. The silence was queer. And where was everyone? It was simply impossible to run an operation of this size with as few workers as Lance had seen since landing. Come to think of it, he hadn't heard a plane take off or land either. How could Zimmer hope to acquire Smith's business when, apparently, there weren't enough contracts to keep this one running?

The hangar was devoid of humanity but there was a trio of planes in various states of maintenance. Engine couplings had been removed from one, another was minus a wing while a third slumped like an eviscerated leviathan against the far wall. Lance risked moving deeper into the hangar to look over these aircraft. A quick inspection shed little light on the mystery.

Everything was ship-shape. Spit and polish right down the line. From the tools to the exposed, greased inner workings of the planes.

There was nothing further to be learned from the place and Lance did not have the time to root around in every corner of the vast structure. A side door let him out across to the living quarters.

He crossed to the stairs leading to the nearest door. Crouching well below the small window set in the door.

Lance raised up and peered through the dusty glass. He saw a narrow cot against one wall, a brown blanket pulled taught across the frame. A simple metal desk was opposite the bed. A half-open closet door between the two. The next door's window showed him a mirror image of the first room.

Lance entered the third room, closest to the offices. He heard muffled voices through the wall. Koller with his Sky Rangers. The occupant of this room was a tinkerer. Splayed out across a drop cloth on the small desk were the inner workings of a clock. A fire extinguisher stood against one leg. The drawers yielding nothing.

Chairs shifted and voices rose in volume next door. What passed for Koller's hospitality had played itself out. He had to abandon the search.

He scurried up to the corner of the building and risked a glance through the skeletal hedge planted there. He saw the backs of the men as they approached the plane. They would get it fixed and in the air in no time.

Lance Star was cut off!

Lance could only watch helplessly while Red led two of Zimmer's men aboard while Buck kept the others occupied.

Lance cast his gaze about for some means of reaching the plane unobserved. His keen eyes fixed on something in the distance and his heart sank. It was a cloud of dust on the road – kicked up by the tires of Zimmer's Duisenberg as it rumbled up to the base. Luckily it was still a few miles off but a supercharged SJ Deusy could really eat up the road and if the driver had her up to her top speed of 140MPH, then Zimmer and more of his henchmen would be arriving much too soon for Lance's liking.

From his hiding place, he tried to catch Buck's eye. The mustached pilot was too engrossed in keeping Koller distracted and did not see Lance as he regaled them with his tales of adventure and waved a foul-smelling, five-cent cigar around. For a second he thought eye contact had been made but

Tellonger's face remained inscrutable and there was no way to be certain.

Light hammering from inside the plane caught Buck's attention, however, and he turned to glance at the open hatch behind him. As he did so, he caught a glimpse of the dust cloud Lance had seen moments before and, like his boss, guessed the meaning. He moved to the plane and leaned his head inside. "Easy, now, fellas. Don't knock the rivets out of her!"

Lance turned his gaze to the cloud. It was larger, closer, and now he could see the black shape of the automobile on the road. Time was running out.

"That's got it!" a voice bellowed from within the aircraft. Lance recognized it as belonging to Red. The man appeared a second later and stepped down to allow Zimmer's men to exit the plane.

"Damn fuel line," Red went on. "She's right as rain."

"You are sure," Koller asked with a concern that was not genuine.

"Yup, she'll fly now."

"Okay, then," Tellonger announced. Lance could tell by their movements that Buck and Davis had worked out a signal amongst themselves – probably that crack about the rivets – to let the other know that it was time to scamper. Lance commended them on their ingenuity as they piled into the ship after thanking Koller for the hospitality.

The Duisenberg was drawing closer every second.

And Lance was no closer to getting aboard the plane than he was five minutes ago.

The engines of the DC-3 coughed and roared. Buck was not wasting any time getting the bird in the air at this point. For a split second he gave the engine too much throttle and a blast of loose sand blown by desert wind onto the tarmac lifted up in twin obscuring clouds.

Buck did it again and this time Lance got the message.

The Duisenberg was at the main gate. The guard there had to step out of the guard house to manually raise the wooden barrier. He was not in a hurry to do so although he still performed the action much quicker than Lance would have preferred.

He tensed. This was going to be close.

Buck got the plane moving – much faster than was necessary – and swung the craft slightly. Zimmer's men were too close. Perfect.

One last look at the auto; it was through the gate, rumbling towards the office building.

Tellonger rammed gas into the engines, the blades whined. A geyser of sand shot up in a blinding cloud. The plane lurched towards Lance's position. He broke and ran for all he was worth.

While Zimmer's men pawed the sand from their shocked faces and tearing eyes, Lance Star ran up to the plane, skirted under the wing and lurched for the hatchway – the door of which had been opened by Red who crouched, an arm extended.

A final lunge. The two men gripped forearms and Lance was hauled aboard. They tumbled to the deck, then scrambled to get the cabin door secured as the plane rocketed down the runway and arced into the air.

The Duisenberg slewed to a halt in front of the sandy men. The doors were flung open. Lance watched all this unfold from the nearest window.

"Hang on a minute," he said. "Hand me those binoculars. Quick!"

Davis had a set around his neck. He wore then in case they had had to look for Lance from above. As this proved unnecessary, he'd forgotten he was wearing them. He yanked them over his flaming head of red hair and thrust them at Lance.

The young aviator drew the binoculars to his eyes and studied the scene below for a moment. He handed the glasses back and led the way up to the cockpit.

"Got him?" Buck asked at the sound of their approach. His eyes were fixed on the controls as the ship rose gracefully.

"Roger that," Lance replied.

"Glad you could make it, Boss," Tellonger said as Lance clapped him on the shoulder.

"Good work with the sand," Lance congratulated the wily pilot. "That was quick thinking."

"It was dicey, I'll give you that," Buck replied. "I spotted you and hoped for the best. But I didn't know if you'd see what I was aiming at when I juiced the engines."

"Came in loud and clear," Lance admitted. "Getting so we can read each other's minds."

"Your stroll around turn up anything, Lance?" Red asked.

"Aside from Zimmer being short staffed, not a thing," Lance replied. "What's Zimmer's game? And why go after Smith's outfit? I'm afraid we came away with more questions than answers, fellas."

"I just wish I could have seen Zimmer's face down there," Buck gloated. "Did anyone get a look at him? I bet that kraut is having kittens about now, wondering what a strange ship was doing on his field while he's away starting trouble."

"Odd about that," Lance breathed.

"What's up, Lance?" Red asked.

"Zimmer wasn't in that jalopy. I watched as they all climbed out. Not a sign of him."

"Where'd he get to?" Buck asked. "There's nothing but desert as far as the eye can see."

"Add that to the growing list of mysteries we're up against," Lance concluded. "Maybe Smith and that odd duck Culver can clear some of this mess up. Open her up, Buck. It's time we got to the bottom of this thing."

It was quite a different reception awaiting them after Buck set the plane down at Smith's field. Culver's men, and this is how Lance and crew thought of them at this point, were out in force – only this time they wore sidearms and carried carbines.

Culver, standing at the head of the group, stepped forward to intercept the aviators as they stepped down into the broiling sun.

"Gentlemen, you will come with me,"

"Hello to you, too," Buck deadpanned. "We did have a bit of trouble but good old American ingenuity got us out of it. Thanks for asking."

Lance gave Tellonger a look to curb further outbursts but it was not needed. Culver's response was to merely turn and walk towards Smith's offices.

The airmen had no choice but to follow along.

After their eyes adjusted to the relative gloom after the brightness outside, they saw Smith glowering behind his chair at the conference table.

Lance turned to Culver but the man was absorbed with laying out three identical documents on the table.

"Sign these please," he said, placing a fountain pen on the center sheet.

Buck's temper flared. "My friend is on the verge of losing his business and you're pushing papers at us?"

"Once this formality has been dispensed with, we can take the next steps together."

"What are we signing?" Lance asked.

"Call it an assurance of confidentiality."

"We signed those when we hooked up with General Pettigrew," Red protested.

Culver nodded. "I know. I had the records pulled and the signatures checked. We have no problem there."

"Now you want us to sign again?" Buck protested. "You were all set to spill the beans before we lit out of here for Zimmer's outfit."

"You were to receive a cover story. Nothing more. Mr. Zimmer's visit has escalated things and security measures must be taken." He motioned to the sheets. "This statement provides you with limited ultra top secret clearance and will supersede the previous document during this operation."

"Lance, he wants us to sign our lives away," Buck complained.

Culver clasped his hands behind his back. "Gentlemen, I believe you are solid citizens. And I believe you want to help your friend. Either sign this document and work with Mr. Smith and myself or get into your planes and go back where you came from. Time is short and decisions have to be made."

Lance Star snorted, then strode to the table. He snatched up the pen and signed the document. This action decided the matter for his associates as they would gladly follow him into the deepest pit of Hell. Buck and Red signed as well. Culver blotted the signatures dry and deposited the documents into a briefcase at his feet. He sat down at the table and motioned Lance and the others to do likewise.

"The next forty-eight hours are critical and nothing that is said or takes place during this time leaves this field," Culver began.

"Watch it," Buck chided. "He's going to get out his pen again."

"This is no laughing matter." Culver waited for silence before continuing. The room grew quiet. "Any of you three familiar with the Devil's Arm?"

"Which one?" Buck asked. "Right or left?"

"Pipe down," Lance instructed. He turned his attention to Culver. "You mean that stretch of desert between Las Vegas and Groom Lake?"

"The same," Culver replied. "But calling it a stretch of desert is like calling the sun just a bright light in the sky."

"What about this Devil's Arm?"

"Fifty years ago, the Land Express Line laid track along the arm, connecting Dry Gulch to Prospector's Promise. It doesn't matter if you've never heard of these places because both are ghost towns now. The track is still intact, however, and still in use."

"For what? If there's nothing out there like you say… "

"There most definitely is something out there, Star," Culver corrected. "The US Army leased that land from the city of Las Vegas for the Groom Lake testing facility."

"And this stretch of track is the way to and from the base," Lance said.

"No, it isn't. At least it's not a route in regular service."

"Either sign, or go back home."

"What in the name of Hell does this have to do with Smitty's air business?" Buck roared.

Culver continued, undaunted. "It has everything to do with Mr. Smith's operation. You see that track carries POTUS to the facility and back annually when the president of the United States inspects the latest experimental craft being tested there. To be clear, let me say the POTUS train crosses the Devil's Arm to the testing ground. The Commander-in-Chief does not."

"POTUS?" Buck inquired.

Culver seemed irritated at the interruption and it showed in the tone of his reply. "That is the designation code railroad dispatchers use for the president's train. An acronym for President of the United States. May I continue?"

"All right, don't get snippy. We're not all up on this cloak and dagger stuff."

"Why can't the president ride the rails?" Red asked, his eyes saucer wide at what he and the others were mixed up in.

"It is standard procedure to order inspections of all track POTUS may use as well as to re-route all rail traffic. If a bridge or length of track is deemed unsafe, then precautions are taken. The Devil's Arm is two hundred and eighty-three miles of open track in the middle of desert as flat as a table top in the middle of nowhere. It is an impossible stretch of track to defend, there are no spur lines to run decoys either. In the darkness of the desert night, anyone could plant explosives anywhere along the line. You see my point, gentlemen."

Realization dawned on Lance's face. "So the train itself is the decoy. It runs as usual but you use Smith to fly President Roosevelt in and out. That's it, isn't it?"

"Precisely," Culver agreed. "However that may be about to change – given recent events."

"Like Hell!" Smith bellowed. "I put my outfit up against any field in the country! It's that Zimmer who is trying to louse things up for me!"

"Where the president's safety is concerned, we deal in evidence, not accusations," Culver explained. "I'll admit that Zimmer is behaving aggressively with regards to acquiring your operation. However that is not a matter of national security."

"Ah, it's as plain as day!" Smith insisted.

"To you, perhaps. My focus is on the president. In the three years since Western Air Express became too prominent for our purposes, Smith Field had done the nation a great service and we are not ungrateful. Your recent setbacks, however, have resulted in a tragic loss of life which cannot be explained away as the result of a competition for clients. You machines, your pilots and your staff are under suspicion and, at present, cannot be relied on."

"It's Zimmer! I ..."

Culver held up a hand to halt Smith's diatribe.

"Whatever is at the heart of the current situation, it does not change the fact that the president will arrive in two days and arrangements must be made. If Smith Field is disqualified, then Mr. Zimmer's field may better suit the president's needs."

"But that's what that kraut wants!"

"Again, Mr. Smith, show me evidence of wrongdoing."

"How does this usually work?" Lance interrupted.

Culver continued without batting an eye. "The president's train reaches Las Vegas at twilight where it stops so that he may address the citizenry before the train continues. Just outside Las Vegas, the train stops and the president is removed. He is driven here and spends the night while the train continues to the facility. Mr. Smith flies the president into the facility at dawn, bypassing the Devil's Arm length of track. After the inspection, the president poses for photographs aboard the train and the air transport process is repeated once photo evidence is obtained to prove that President Roosevelt travels only by rail."

Lance thought over the security measures he and his crew had been put through just to get to this point. There was only one conclusion to be drawn.

"If what Smith says is true, and Zimmer wants to steal this contract for himself, then how did he find out about it in the first place? Who talked?"

"This country is not without its enemies." Culver shrugged. "If Zimmer is aware of the arrangement, we will have to be determined how he found out after this crisis is passed."

"It was none of my men!" Smith bellowed.

"Gentlemen, lets us stay on point. The president needs a ride."

"Buck? Star?" Smith pleaded. "Didn't you find out anything?"

Lance recounted his search of Zimmer's field and the exemplary state of the facility. He expressed his suspicions about the few staff at the field however. Buck and Red had nothing to add to that except that what staff they met couldn't get rid of them fast enough.

Culver's brow clouded. "My advance teams looked over Zimmer's field and gave it an A-1 rating. Another inspection is in order it seems. I have superiors I must answer to and this is how they want things to be done."

"It's your time to waste," Red observed.

"The US government does not waste time," Culver responded. "I will get my people together and head out there first thing tomorrow."

Lance Star awoke from a restful sleep as dawn spread across the horizon. It was the sound of an airplane engine turning over that woke him and to Lance there was no better sound to start the day with. He climbed out of the cot he'd fallen into last night and, clad in an undershirt and shorts, stepped outside.

The morning air was cold, invigorating against his exposed skin. He sucked in great lungfuls of the chill, morning air. After the meeting had broken up, there was nothing more they could do at the moment so far as Zimmer was concerned. So he, Buck and Red had helped Smith with the day-to-day operation of the field since Smith was a pilot down. Buck had flown into Tucson for parts while Red put his mechanical expertise to good use, helping out Smith's staff in not only keeping the birds flying but also to ensure that neither Zimmer nor his men had left any other surprises in the wake of the exploding engine earlier.

Lance had flown two missions himself. The first was to ferry a Smith staffer with a cracked rib to Vegas for treatment and the other to shakedown the new DC-3 in the hope the president would be using it soon. The evening's activities had gone off without a hitch, returning some semblance of calm to the anxious operation.

As Lance shook the last cobwebs of sleep out of his mind, he ambled towards the idling plane. The sun had yet to crest the horizon but there was enough light for him to see that the plane preparing for take off was the mail skipper bound for the transfer station where the letter sacks would be passed over to the next link in the chain between Vegas and Flagstaff. Pilot Pete Sinclair had left their brief bull session last night to turn in early for the sake of this run.

From his spot leaning against the hangar wall, he watched the ground's crew remove the chocks then step well back out of the draft generated by the propeller, light cigarettes and give a wave to the pilot before ducking inside to grab some breakfast. Lance just made out Sinclair's profile as the pilot gave them a thumbs up through the open side window

As Lance turned away, with thoughts of breakfast all-encompassing, he caught a glimpse of a man jogging towards the plane's hatch. At the moment the runner's face became visible the sun crested the horizon and shone in Lance's face, blinding him. Through the glare he saw this second Sinclair yank open the hatch and scrabble inside. Thinking his eyes were playing tricks on him in the dodgy morning light, Lance headed back, convinced the last minute arrival had to have been Sinclair's co-pilot delayed by a sleepy head or the need to relieve himself. The siren song of hot coffee, eggs and bacon soon got the better of him and he put all thought of what had just transpired out of his mind. The plane picked up speed, left the ground and cleaved the morning air. Buck and Red joined him at breakfast a few minutes later and dug in.

Their amiable meal was suddenly interrupted when Smith burst into the cafeteria with deadly news.

"There's been a crash!"

With lives at stake, it was time for action. The Sky Rangers leapt out of their seats and followed Smith outside. The field chief stopped them as they made a bee line for the Skybolt II, barking to them that the plane had gone down in sand and the truck was their best bet. They piled inside as Smith gunned the engine and slammed the gear home.

"What do you know?" Lance asked at last as the truck skidded out onto the road.

"I had the field glasses out and was scanning the horizon for weather," Smith began, his hands clutched on the wheel, his piercing gaze straight ahead. "It does happen, even in the desert. I didn't see the plane hit but I saw the flame when the fuel went. It was out by the sand plain at the foot of the Cochise range."

"If this crate'll take more, feed it!" Buck urged. If the plane had come down in sand, there was a better chance the pilot might walk away with a whole skin. Every second was precious.

The column of thick, black smoke guided them in. Smith stood on the brakes and the truck slewed. Lance and the others were out and sprinting towards the crash before the truck came to a halt. The loose sand flew up at their heels as they dashed headlong.

What they saw stopped them dead in their tracks.

The plane was burning fiercely. Anyone inside was beyond reach.

Smith exited the truck with a fire extinguisher in his hands. He pumped the device and white foam sprayed over the blackened fuselage. In minutes the fire was out.

Gingerly they approached the smouldering cockpit. The plane had skimmed into the sand and aside from the fire and shattered glass, the craft was in one piece. Doing his best to ignore the stench of burnt flesh, Lance peered through the smoky glass. What he saw made him wish he'd skipped breakfast. Seconds later, it was if he had.

Smith was on the other side of the cockpit and had a similar reaction. He jumped down to the sand and collapsed.

Buck saw to the grisly work of extracting the pilot's remains while Lance did his best to comfort the bereaved Smith.

"Pete Sinclair, my best friend," Smith intoned, the knuckles of one hand pounding rhythmically against his forehead.

"There's something not right about this," Red observed. "That craft was tip-top, Lance. I checked it over with Smith's people before dawn. A sure-fire airplane in the hands of an ace like Sinclair... there's no way this bird ditches. We're missing something."

"My best goddamn friend in the world – cooked like that!" Smith went on, oblivious to Red's musings. "How am I going to explain it to his wife?"

Lance made a motion to Davis with his head, indicating that the mechanic aid Buck with the body, then stood over Smith and gripped his shoulder. "Are you sure that's Sinclair? She came in soft and that glass is broken out. Maybe Sinclair scrambled out."

"You saw what's left of him!"

Lanced glanced over at the charred remains lying on the sand at the rear of the truck. Red had hopped onto the truck bed to retrieve a tarp. He handed it to Buck before jumping down to help wrap the corpse, which hardly appeared human.

"You can't be sure," Lance explained. "That could be the co-pilot laying there."

Smith raised his tear-stained face and glared at Lance. "What in hell are you talking about?"

"The body. It could be the co-pilot." Lance glanced at the wrecked plane. It's a chance in a million someone made it out of there but we have to be sure."

"Sinclair flew alone," Smith corrected. "He always flew alone. He had more hours in the air than most have on the ground."

Lance was taken aback. "I saw two men aboard that plane. Before she took off. I was taking some air and saw the bird head out."

"And I'm telling you you're wrong," Smith insisted. "Sinclair wouldn't stand for a co-pilot. He'd have burst into my office chewing ten-penny nails if anyone even suggested it. He would not have lifted off with a co-pilot."

"I'll prove it." Lance stepped up onto the tilted wing rammed into the loose sand and climbed up to the cockpit.

Aside from the fire damage, the plane was more or less intact as the sea of sand in this part of the desert had cushioned the impact. If the ship had had a little more air under her she would have pancaked against the mountain range towering above them a half-mile east of the wreck.

Defying the stench of roasted flesh, Lance peered through the sooty, cracked glass at the two pilot seats. One was charred, belching padding like lard. The other bore similar scars but the instrument panel, seat cushion and controls were coated in seared black – as if some liquid had sprayed over them seconds before the fire.

Sudden realization dawned on Lance. "Hold up, guys!" he called to Buck and Red finishing up their grim task. He rose up from his haunches, dropped down off the wing and joined them. Crouching he pulled the tarp free from the head of the corpse. Gagging, he inspected the hideous remains.

It was then that Lance new. He lowered the tarp, then straightened.

"Brothers," he addressed his men. "Use this jalopy to backtrack the plane's path. Scour every inch of desert for half a mile."

Tellonger took the strange request in stride. "What are we looking for?"

"A parachute," Lance replied. "And tire tracks. Get going. I'll finish up here."

The truck roared away a minute later. Lance finished wrapping Sinclair's body, then rejoined Smith. "On your feet, friend," he ordered. "I'm sorry for your loss but there's a chance at seeing those responsible pay."

"I don't read you," Smith began, haltingly. "The plane. It crashed. Sinclair…"

"Pull yourself together if you want to save your friend's reputation. Sinclair didn't crash this bird. He was murdered beforehand."

"What are you saying?"

"There's charred blood all over the pilot's panel and on the seat we found Sinclair in. The co-pilot's chair was clean."

"I told you…"

"And I'm telling you I saw two men aboard this plane. Your friend's throat has been cut. Ear to ear."

"The crash," Smith spluttered. "Flying glass… "

"That was my first thought. But the cut is too clean. Whoever I saw sneak aboard that plane just before takeoff slit Sinclair's throat."

"And committed suicide in the process?" Smith was sceptical. "You're crazy."

Lance saw the truck returning. They'd not had time to search the entire area and he concluded they must be returning early because they had found something. At least that was his hope.

It was a hope well-founded. As the truck drew closer, Lance saw the end of the parachute flapping in the backwash from where it dangled over the edge of the truck bed.

"We found it!" Red whooped as Buck braked the truck and killed the engine. "You were right, Lance!" Davis sprang out of the vehicle and rushed to his friend. "Whoever left it did a rush job trying to hide that chute. We spotted it right off."

Tellonger had joined them by this point. "We found tire tracks as well, Lance. What's it all about?"

"Those tracks? Wide-chassis?" Lance asked. "Deep?"

"Yes to all of that," Red replied. "How do you figure it?"

"Sinclair had a stowaway," Lance explained. "I saw him board but thought he was the co-pilot at first. Turns out Sinclair never flew with one. So the second man was there to kill Sinclair. He slit the pilot's throat, then bailed out over a waiting auto." He turned his gaze to Smith. "You say Sinclair flew the mail at the same time, every week?"

"Like clockwork," Smith replied. "Cooky used to hold his breakfast for him"

"There it is," Lance said, simply.

Tellonger and Davis took a few moments to let it all sink in. It was Red who spoke first. "Okay, I'll buy it. We've really stepped in it this time, boyo. But, Lance, you say you saw the second man. Can you identify him?"

"The sun was in my eyes."

"Then, we're sunk," Red said.

"No," Lance countered. "Remember what happened to that ship Jet Garcia was flying?"

"It crashed into a mountain," Buck said.

"Exactly. And this one just missed doing likewise. The winds must play the devil with aircraft here. Right, Smith?"

Smith nodded, his thoughts churning.

"I thought so with all this loose sand," Lance continued. "And that's where the murderer slipped up. He snuck aboard, slit Sinclair's throat, then jumped clear. The ship, with a dying man at the controls, was supposed to crash into the Cochise mountains where piecing together what really happened would be all but impossible with wreckage strewn for miles around."

"Like that passenger plane," Buck added.

"Now you've got it. Only the wind brought this bird down early. Or maybe Sinclair had enough fight in him to ease her down short of the range. Either way, the evidence of foul play the killer hoped to obliterate remained intact. Add to that the parachute and the tracks of the getaway car out here in the middle of nowhere and its murder sure as you're standing there."

"Okay, that tracks," Tellonger admitted. "You figure Zimmer for this?"

"Aside from Culver, who here has a background in cloak and dagger work? Remember we didn't see him with his men when that Deusy returned. He must have snuck back in to Smith's field to hole up until dawn when he knew Sinclair would be heading out."

"Wait 'til I get my hands on that kraut!" Smith threatened.

"Not if I find him first!" Buck stated.

"Hold your horses," Lance soothed. "It's a strong case that's weak on facts. We know Zimmer has been trying to run Smith out of business and that the setbacks began with Zimmer's presence. The man does have an espionage background and could be practiced in the art of infiltration. Those heavy, wide-bodied tracks I asked you about could have been made by a Deusy. But all we know for sure was that Zimmer had a motive, the opportunity and the means to make this play. We need hard evidence if we're going to make a charge stick."

"We'll get it!" Red insisted. "But what's Zimmer's end game? Would he go through all this just to steal Smith's business?"

"The presidential contract," Smith replied. "That's what this is all about."

"Still," Davis said. "Zimmer wouldn't go about wholesale murder just for the right to fly the president around for a day."

"You couldn't be more right, Red," Lance agreed. "I think getting close to the president has been Zimmer's end all along. We've got to get back. If we're right about all this, the president is in grave danger!"

They returned to learn that Culver and his team had already departed for their inspection of Zimmer's field. After seeing to Sinclair's body, they gathered in the staff room to hash out their next move but ultimately their hands were tied until Culver and his team returned.

The hours passed like centuries. Half a dozen times, Lance was tempted to hop aboard the Skybolt II and wing it out to stop Zimmer from soft soaping Culver and his crew. There was no point to it; really, as he knew Zimmer's men wouldn't allow him onto the base at this stage of the game.

And so they waited. When the sun finally waned and the day's work was done, the field settled down to an uneasy stillness. The temperature dipped and Lance followed Smith outside with Buck and Red in tow.

The sound of the automobile roused them and they stepped off the low porch and into the indigo twilight to intercept Culver and party. They'd learned that Culver had taken his entire staff with him – a dozen men along with their leader making a group of thirteen – which was why the lone auto with just Culver and a driver took them by surprise.

"Gentlemen," Culver said as he stepped out of the vehicle. His features grew grave. "That trouble this morning... "

Smith had no choice but to tell the Secret Service man about what they'd found.

"A terrible tragedy," Culver summarized. "And I'm afraid I have more bad news, Mr. Smith. I have selected Zimmer's outfit to transport POTUS. Events here left me no choice."

The news shocked Lance and his men into stunned silence. Finally Lance said. "You're making a mistake."

"Give us some credit, Mr. Star."

"Star is right," Smith interjected. "Zimmer has set up this whole thing."

"So you keep saying," Culver condescended. "However I told you I would consider evidence."

Lance gripped Culver by the elbow. "We've got evidence... of a sort."

"Of a sort?" the government man echoed.

Lance snorted, visibly trying to calm himself. "If you'll just give us a chance to lay it out for you. The president isn't due to arrive until tomorrow after all. Hear us out. You owe us, and him, that much."

"I'm afraid that's impossible. You see, with security here under suspicion, I deliberately withheld the truth. President Roosevelt is already at Zimmer Field. My men are helping him and his son get settled. I returned here to collect my effects and any documentation in Mr. Smith's possession. In the morning, Zimmer will personally fly the president to the testing grounds."

⌐

Lance and the other followed Culver into his quarters. The man pulled a suitcase from under the bed and began feeding clothes into it.

"You've given Zimmer precisely what he wants: access to the president," Lance began. "We're convinced the man committed multiple murders to achieve this." Lance explained their findings to Culver who, to his credit, listened attentively.

"So it's your contention that Zimmer crashed two planes, murdered more than a dozen people all to discredit Mr. Smith so that we would bring POTUS to him?"

"Exactly that."

"Well, it's outlandish to say the least. Look, I'll admit that the rash of, shall we say, bad luck, Mr. Smith experienced is not above suspicion. However, I need evidence, gentlemen, not conclusions." He snapped the bag closed.

Lance's mind raced as he searched for something that would convince Culver as they returned to the automobile. "Answer me this, was Zimmer present during your inspection? We hold that he was aboard that mail carrier. He couldn't be in two places at once, right? If he was at the field, if you saw him there with your own eyes, then that would clear a lot up."

Culver smiled. "I wish I could say that he was there but he was not."

"There you go!" Buck blurted.

"I did speak to him on the telephone however. We were told that he had injured his ankle while inspecting the plane reserved for the president before we arrived, and had to be taken to Las Vegas for x-rays."

"And you swallowed that?" Lance asked. "That was clearly a cover story for an injury sustained during his hasty exit out of that mail plane after murdering Sinclair. The president is in danger."

"Nothing could be further from the truth," Culver contradicted. "I'm afraid Mr. Zimmer's ankle is broken. The man will not be doing any malicious skulking. He certainly poses no threat in his current condition. Now if you'll excuse me."

Lance, Tellonger and Davis stood by the auto while Smith and Culver disappeared into Smith's office. They conspired in harsh whispers but there seemed no way of convincing Culver of Zimmer's guilt. When the secret service man emerged from the office, Lance had an idea.

"All right, Culver, I've got a solution here," Lance said. "You've seen my clearances, right?" Culver nodded. "Fine. Let me be Zimmer's co-pilot on tomorrow's flight."

"I need evidence, gentlemen, not conclusions."

Culver placed a sheaf of papers on the passenger seat of the auto as he considered Lance's proposal. "I'm certain Mr. Zimmer would reject such a suggestion."

"I have no doubt he will," Lance agreed. "But you don't take orders from Mr. Zimmer, do you?"

"Come on," Buck urged. "Lance is the best pilot in the country. If you want to ensure the president survives the flight, doesn't it make sense to have the best man at the stick?"

"Call it an extra layer of security," Lance added.

Culver sighed, his mind made up. "That, gentlemen, is the first sound suggestion I've heard here tonight." Culver climbed into the car and spoke through the open window. "Hop in, Mr. Star. We've got a busy night ahead of us."

The protests of Buck and Red over Lance going into the lion's den alone still ringing in his ears, the young aviator's mind churned as the car approached Zimmer's air field. Lance had replied to Buck that he was leaving the Skybolt II in the pilot's capable hands and could only hope the man got the message implied in the statement.

Zimmer's field was a hive of activity. There was a slight delay at the gate when the identity of Culver's passenger was relayed to Zimmer's underlings but it was the former German ace himself who eventually got on the line, instructing them to join him in Hangar One.

The German was not hard to spot. Tall, regal and sporting a shining white cast on his right ankle, Zimmer hobbled about a Curtiss YC-30 Condor II being worked on by his staff while Secret Service agents scrutinized every action. Zimmer turned at the sound of their engine and worked the crutches to meet them as the car pulled up.

"Herr Culver, a pleasure to see you again," Zimmer said. "I've sent away all but essential personnel as an added precaution."

"Mr. Star will fly with you tomorrow," Culver explained, then said. "As an added precaution."

Zimmer turned to Lance. "The intrepid Lance Star! I have been made aware of your exploits. Welcome."

Lance grimaced and did not offer to shake the German's hand. Zimmer knew he and the Rangers had been here. And that line about reducing staff was hogwash. The men had never existed. Lance was certain now that Zimmer had carefully orchestrated everything to bring the president here and that the attempt to steal Smith's contracts was a mere ruse.

The formalities dispensed with, Zimmer lead them into Hangar One so Culver could see how the preparations for the flight were going. What followed were hours of careful inspection. The Condor II had her every inch repeatedly scrutinized. Every rivet was checked along her fifty feet of length and her eighty-two foot wingspan. The ship boasted numerous access panels to allow workers to get at any part of the plane but these now had guards posted around them. Lance questioned the use of a fabric shell over an aluminum frame to protect the Commander-in-Chief but Cuvler explained to him that the president did not fly often, and until an official plane could be designated for POTUS' use, secrecy was the best protection. The inspection continued long into the night.

Sleep would have been ideal in preparation for the dawn flight but Lance could not afford to let Zimmer out of his sight. The president had retired for some much needed rest Lance was told. He knew how Zimmer operated even though he could not prove it to Culver's satisfaction and set about looking over the German's shoulder as the plane was checked and re-checked. Hobbled by the thick cast and crutches, Zimmer was still able to be everywhere at once, putting on a show of diligence, Lance knew, for Culver and his men.

Dawn came and Lance rubbed at his tired eyes, remembering the previous morning and another plane about to depart. He was painfully reminded of how that flight had turned out and whose hand he was certain had spelled doom for Sinclair. This time there would be no surprises.

When the air horn sounded it did not startle Lance. Culver had drilled the procedure into their heads and he knew what to do. The Secret Service man had made it perfectly clear that everyone except himself and the presidential detail were to gather in Hangar Two to wait while the president boarded the waiting plane in Hangar One. No reason was given for this other than that it was a matter of national security.

Lance, who was in Hangar One when the blast cut the air, sidled out to the neighbouring hangar where Zimmer's men were already gathered. He ignored the dirty looks aimed his way as he mingled with the crowd. His head turned this way and that in search of Zimmer and spotted the big German at the opposite end.

"The games you Americans play," Zimmer said by way of greeting.

"I don't follow you," Lance replied. "If anyone is playing games here it's you. Deadly games."

Zimmer seemed genuinely amused. "You really don't know your president, do you?"

"What kind of crack is that?"

Zimmer just smiled.

The horn sounded again. The president was on board.

Lance and Zimmer made their way to Hangar One. The Secret Service agents posted at the entry to the hangar let them pass. The rest of Zimmer's men stayed put. Lance tensed, every nerve tingling. It was crunch time now. Whatever Zimmer was planning would take place in the air. Lance knew that much. The government agents had the hangar sewn up tight, allowing only the two pilots to approach the aircraft. Lance needed to be ready for anything.

The snub-nosed, twin-engine Condor II bi-plane loomed before them with a circle of agents around it. The large craft usually boasted a crew of three but for this flight only Lance and Zimmer would be at the controls. The pilots were frisked at the hatch by two stone-face agents who then stepped aside to let them go aboard. Lance let Zimmer go first and did not offer to help the man as he struggled with his crutches.

Culver was waiting for them. "Gentlemen, let's have a smooth flight. The less bumps for the president, the better."

Lance gazed down the length of the craft and saw President Roosevelt at the rear, seated at a collapsible conference table, surrounded by his son, James, and two aides. The president was deep in conversation and did not look up as the pilots entered. The cabin door was secured.

Lance dropped into the left pilot's seat without asking Zimmer. It was the obvious choice anyway as the German could not work the pedals with that cast. Zimmer stowed his crutches took the co-pilot's seat.

"That was some creative flying you and Sinclair pulled off yesterday," Lance said as he worked the controls.

"I have no idea what you are talking about."

"Yes, you do," Lance insisted. "I don't know how many you've killed to get to this point, but it ends here. That's my Commander-in-Chief back there and I'll be damned if I'll let you get your grubby paws on him. Get me?"

"Are we here to fly or palaver?" Zimmer asked. There was a malicious glint in his eye.

"I'll show you some flying," Lance assured.

The two men were consummate professionals, checking over the instrument panels as a trio of Secret Service agents outside observed Zimmer's staff as the plane was walked into the morning air.

The engines growled to life under Lance's ministrations. The Condor was ready to fly. Lance waited for Culver to pound twice on the cockpit door to indicate that the president was ready. They were clear for take off.

Lance fed fuel to the engines and the 650HP engines roared lustily. With a look of grim determination on his young face, Lance got the plane moving. The plane barrelled down the runway and lifted gracefully into the frigid morning air, climbing rapidly to twenty-three thousand feet.

The first few minutes of the flight were routine. Zimmer gave Lance their course and the American double-checked it before turning the ship. Muffled conversation reached them through the cockpit door, then dropped off as the plane settled on course. It was still very early in the day and the last hours had been fraught with activity. Lance wouldn't begrudge any of the passengers a quick forty winks, all things considered.

Lance could not afford to let his guard down. Not with Zimmer sitting across from him and President Roosevelt aboard.

Zimmer, for his part, seemed to be waiting for something. He used a slide rule to get at the itch caused by the cast. This simple human need almost made Lance forget the deaths the man seated beside him had caused.

Then Zimmer bent over, snapped the fake cast open and withdrew a small revolver and a stiletto knife.

He slashed at Lance with the knife as he swung the gun up. Lance caught the movement from the corner of his eye and jerked his hand off the stick to block the knife thrust.

"Verfluchte Amerikaner!" Zimmer swore as his initial attack was diverted.

The plane quivered as Lance flew it one-handed. As he saw Zimmer point the gun at him awkwardly, Lance swivelled in his seat and brought his right foot up to kick at the German's gun hand. The manoeuvre worked as Lance pinned Zimmer's hand against the control panel.

Zimmer thought fast. Snarling, he fought to free his knife hand. But this was just a feint. Angling the pistol, he emptied the magazine into the control panel. Sparks flew amidst pieces of shrapnel from the exploding controls. The plane went into a nose dive.

Lance lashed out with the foot that had been holding the gun, catching

Zimmer in the chest and slamming him against the cockpit window.

"Culver!" Lance bellowed.

There was no response. How had the passengers not heard the gunshots?

Lance launched at Zimmer who was fighting to catch his breath. "What have you done?"

"Merely... set... the... stage... "

With that he stabbed at Lance again and the blade went through his open jacket. Lance grabbed the material and twisted before Zimmer could withdraw the blade and the stiletto clattered to the deck.

Lance drove a fist into Zimmer's face and blood exploded from mashed lips. Zimmer pistol-whipped Lance, driving him back.

"Kill me or save the President," Zimmer said. "Your choice."

The ground now filled the front windows as the plane plummeted. At their angle of descent the engines would stall any minute. But, dammit, it was time Zimmer got his!

The German ace read the look in Lance's eye and lunged forward. The two pilots locked in deadly combat. Lance knocked the empty pistol from Zimmer's hand but received two piston-like jabs to the face in the process. Lance stomped on the man's right instep with his boot heel. Zimmer roared in agony and reared back.

Exactly what Lance had been hoping for. He managed a roundhouse swing in the close confines and it connected with Zimmer's jaw. It was not enough to lay the man out but the force of the blow drove Zimmer's head back into the controls jutting down out of the planes roof. In rearing up, the back of Zimmer's head was inches from the box and both connected with a meaty thump. Zimmer went limp, sprawling across Lance's prone form.

Lance fought like a wild man to free himself as the ship fell like a stone. Finally he heaved Zimmer's unconscious form off and lunged at the stick. Dead. He scrabbled over Zimmer's body and seized the co-pilot's stick.

The stick was responsive!

Using every bit of his flying experience, Lance coaxed the Condor out of its dive. The engines coughed, spluttered as he fed them fuel. Sprawled across the two seats, arms locked on the other stick while his feet manipulated the flaps from the pilot's chair, Lance fought to get the craft under control.

The plane responded, lifting, but all he saw through the windshield was the desert floor. He worked frantically, sweat standing out on his brow as he used his strength to haul the plane out of danger. The horizon appeared in front of him. He pulled harder and was rewarded with blue sky. The plane levelled off.

Collapsing back against the seat rest, Lance let out the breath he hadn't been aware he was holding.

Reaching over he locked the controls so he could see about Zimmer. The German was still out. Lance made sure the man wasn't faking by planting a boot in the man's groin. Zimmer didn't flinch.

Lance grabbed the German by the scruff of the neck and dragged him to the cockpit door. He flung it open and bundled Zimmer through it.

The passengers sprawled all over the ship. And they were all as dead to the world as Zimmer. Only the president was seated, strapped in, head lolling at the rear of the plane. Lance couldn't understand it. Had they all fainted during the excitement?

He ripped down a curtain cord to bind Zimmer. Lance got one loop around the man's wrist when his vision blurred and he felt dizzy. He reeled back against the bulkhead. A low hissing sounded nearby.

Blackness edged in at the corners of his vision as he flung his head about in search of the source of the noise. All he saw was a fire extinguisher bolted to the wall.

The same one he'd seen with the dismantled clock during his first visit to the Zimmer's field.

The canister was hissing. Knockout gas!

Zimmer had had one of his men fill the extinguisher with the gas and rig a timer. Lance lunged to close the canister valve before staggering back into the cockpit and slamming the door. He collapsed into the pilot's seat and drew a hand across his face as he fought to clear his mind. Shaking his head, his vision cleared and he opened the plane's fans. This allowed cold air to enter the body of the craft and was intended as a cooling measure on hot days. He knew it would expel the gas.

He turned his attention to the state of the aircraft. There was no telling what damage the gunfire had done. Lance didn't even know if he'd be able to land the thing. He disengaged the autopilot. The instrument panel erupted in sparks and smoke coiled out of the bullet holes.

The fuel gauges went dead. He feared the implications of this.

Hastily he banked the plane into a 360 degree turn, scanning the horizon. There! Sun glinted off silver. Tellonger had gotten his message and the Skybolt II was in the air, paralleling the Condor's course. What bothered him was that the mad gyrations the plane had just gone through had not prompted a radio message from Buck.

Lance found the answer to this mystery a moment later. The radio was dead.

Lance waggled the Condor's wings, indicating that Tellonger should draw closer.

That was when the port engine sputtered and died.

Lance's fear about the gauges had come to pass. There was plenty of fuel in the tanks but it was no long reaching the engines.

The Condor began to lose altitude.

The Skybolt II came alongside. With hand signals, Lance explained the mechanical difficulties and Buck nodded from the other cockpit.

Suddenly, Tellonger motioned towards the Condor's cabin door. Lance locked the controls again and burst through the cockpit door. He was just in time to see Zimmer, revived by the freezing air streaming through the cabin, launch himself out into the morning air. A parachute billowed a few seconds later.

Lance was about to gesture to Buck that he should make sauerkraut out of Zimmer's chute with the Skybolt II's propellers but open access panels on the floor of the plane drew his eye. The nearest had held the concealed parachute. But the other... Pitching headlong, Lance gazed into the second hole and cold sweat ran down his backbone.

The rear flap cables had been severed. A pocket knife lay nearby.

Lance sealed the cabin door and bolted to the cockpit. He cut off the cooling airflow to the cabin. The gas was gone along with Zimmer. Then he signalled this new development to Buck who shook his head. How was Lance going to land the Condor with only partial flaps and one engine?

Lance got an idea.

He gestured his intentions to Buck who made him repeat them. Lance did so, hastily. The Condor was continuing to lose altitude.

Tellonger nodded once, his mouth a hard line. Then the Skybolt II banked away. Lance waited anxiously for a minute. Buck returned and pointed to a stretch of desert on the right, then pointed at the Condor and shook his head. Lance nodded.

He banked the Condor gingerly saw the stretch of sand Buck had found. They were going to take a lesson from Sinclair's book and skid the Condor down on to what they hoped was a thick blanket of loose sand like a stone skimming across a still pond.

Only it wouldn't be quite that simple. The starboard engine died. His ship would not have the lift to reach the sand runway.

There was no turning back now. All that remained was one desperate gamble. Lance signalled Buck Tellonger.

Buck and Lance locked eyes and the older airman raised his eyebrows questioningly.

Lance scowled and shook his head. They were committed.

Tellonger dipped the Skybolt II below the Condor.

Lance tried to keep his plane level while he waited for Buck to match speed. It was a credit to Tellonger's abilities that Lance barely felt the first bump when the Skybolt II collided with the Condor's underbelly. There was another scrape, louder and more prolonged this time, then Lance felt his craft lift slightly. Buck had done it!

The plan was daring, dangerous and foolhardy but it was their only option and the life of the president was at stake. What Lance had signalled, and Buck executed to perfection, was for the pilot to get under the Condor and use the Skybolt II's fuselage to cradle the belly of the larger plane. Success depended on whether the re-enforced, boxlike body of the Skybolt II could support the partial weight of the Condor, keeping it aloft long enough to reach the sand.

The sand runway drew closer. Lance and Buck used every trick they knew to keep both craft flying as Buck reduced speed to slow the gliding Condor down. As the anxious minutes passed, gravity fought to pull the Condor from the sky and the strain on the Skybolt II began to reach critical levels.

Finally the plane could stand no more and Tellonger dropped the plane free of its burden. It was up to Lance now as his ship raced towards the sand. The wind was good, the approach the best Buck could manage. If the sand was deep enough, the Condor had a good chance. If not...

The ship struck. A jarring blow that bounced the occupants around inside. The plane skipped, then struck again. Plumes of sand arced out on either side of the plane. This time the plane did not escape the sand's embrace. The nose burrowed through the dry powdery sand, the plane slowed while its fuselage groaned, cracked, yet held together.

As abruptly as it had begun, it was over. Lance rose groggily out of his seat. A gash above one eyebrow bled heavily and he was certain he'd busted a rib in the jostling. His main concern was for the president, however, and he hurried through the cockpit door.

The odor of fuel was everywhere. The slightest spark and the ship would go up. Lance sprinted to the rear of the plane past the passengers. Lance reached the president's side. Roosevelt was awake, shaken up and groggy.

"Hang on, sir," Lance said. "I'll get you out of here in a second."

Lance saw the strange array of straps that held the president in place. It was these restraints that had most likely saved the man's life as the plane skipped across the desert. He did not understand their presence but he was grateful for them. He drew Zimmer's stiletto from his belt and cut the straps away. He then left the president's side to get the cabin door open, then called, "its safe, sir. Follow me!"

The president didn't move.

"Mr. President, this baby could go up any second," Lance urged.

President Roosevelt shook the last cobwebs of the gas from his mind and regarded Lance plainly.

Lance came up the aisle and kneeled at the president's side. "Are you injured, sir?" Without waiting for a reply, he felt the president's legs. They were thin as broom handles. He looked into the president's eyes as realization dawned on him.

"Son," President Roosevelt said. "I'm afraid I'll have to call on your good graces."

Lance understood.

"See to the others first, if you please."

"With all due respect, sir, this plane is not safe. I'm getting you out." Bending, he lifted the president up into his arms and carried him up the aisle and out of the plane. He set the man down against a piece of wing that had sheered off.

President Roosevelt looked at the wreck, then back at Lance. "Hell of a landing, Mr. Star."

"Thank you, Mr. President."

Lance had the rest of the president's entourage out moments later. Culver was awake but could only mumble. One of the Secret Service agents had broken his neck in the jostling and was dead. A shattered collarbone and two broken arms were the extent of the other injuries.

Lance rejoined the president. "Your son is fine, sir. Just knocked out. One of your men didn't make it but the rest are okay."

"What the devil happened?" the president asked.

Lance Star recapped the events for President Roosevelt. From what they knew about Zimmer to the man's plan to cloak an assassination behind an air crash. He finished his report, saying, "I'm afraid Zimmer got away. The desert might claim him. There's no way to know. My associates have landed at the base by now and will be directing the rescue efforts. It won't be long now, sir."

"Excellent, we are in your debt. You've cleared Mr. Smith of any wrongdoing as well and should I consent to fly again the next time I'm here, it will be via his outfit. To think that damned Culver assured me that flying would be safer than the train," Roosevelt said, and both men laughed. Then his tone grew conspiratorial. "I can count on you, son?" He glanced at his legs.

"Without question, sir."

The president nodded "I knew it. Be aware that I conceal my condition from the American people not out of shame but out of necessity. At this time, with the world on the brink of war, the office I hold must convey strength."

"I understand perfectly, sir." Lance now understood the closed hangar when the president had come aboard. He recalled all of the newsreels he'd seen over the years and realized now that the president was always seated in a car or at a table. When standing, he always had his arms linked through those of his sons. Sure, he had heard mention that the president's health was not ideal but he, like so many others, had no idea the man needed a wheelchair to get around.

The sound of approaching engines reached them. Help had arrived.

Secret Service men leapt from the moving vehicles and set up a protective circle around the president. Culver was fully awake now and barked orders. James Roosevelt was also up and around and was at his father's side in a heartbeat. Lance stepped aside to let them do their jobs.

Buck and Red joined him.

Tellonger whooped. "That was some flying! I'd like to see any two other pilots pull that off! And the life of the president in the balance! Can you beat that?"

"How are they going to convince the press at the base that the president came in by train?" Red asked as he watched the group gathered around Roosevelt.

"Culver will think of something," Lance replied. "He's good at that."

A path was cleared as Roosevelt's son carried his father to a waiting car.

"What's up?" Buck hissed to Lance as James Roosevelt scooped his father up in his arms. "Did the president bust a leg or something?"

Lance shook his head and smiled knowingly. "There's nothing that'll slow him down. They're just being careful is all."

"I read you. It's just queer seeing him carried like that."

Lance regarded Buck frankly. "He stands pretty tall in my book. Our work here is done. Buck, Red, let's go home."

THE END

TAKING TO THE SKIES

Some tales seem to write themselves. The words fly along, the pages mount up and before you know it, you're done.

My Lance Star tale was not one of those.

Don't get me wrong. I was thrilled to be invited to contribute a tale to this new volume. I was a fan. Bobby Nash and Airship 27 have done a fantastic job in launching the hero and his Sky Rangers and there have been some great stories in the first three volumes. So I jumped in with both feet and welcomed the challenge of trying to write a tale that was worthy to stand beside those of the other creators.

My tale started off with a bang. The opening scene popped into my head and I couldn't get it down fast enough. I thought I was off and running. Then I hit the wall.

Maybe it was writer's block, which I've never experienced before, or maybe it was the crush of other tales I was working on at the same time, but suddenly, after that first section, Lance and his Sky Rangers were just... gone. I'd lost the handle I had on the story and whenever I put my mind to it I would draw a blank. I didn't know what happened next even though I knew what happened next – if you get what I mean. Oh, I had the overall plot of an assassination attempt on President Roosevelt, I'd completed my research on Lance, FDR and aviation during the time period. All my ducks were in a row, but I could not answer the question: What happens next?

Gradually my muse took pity on me and the story got going again. But the tale would only come in spurts of a few hundred or maybe a thousand words at a time. Whenever I finished a day's work on it, I still could not answer the question above. I simply did not know what happened next. As this is not my usual way of working, it was quite distressing but also an interesting experience. Like the reader, I would have to just follow along to see where the tale was going. Plot ideas I had at the beginning fell by the wayside, new ones replaced them and, over the course of five months, the tale was finally done.

And I'm very satisfied with how it came out. As this was my first ever aviation adventure there was a bit of trepidation going in but I think the tale has enough aerial daring-do to get the job done. I like the plot, too and couldn't resist leaving the fate of the Sky Reaper open in case another writer wants to pit him against Lance and the Sky Rangers in the future.

My thanks go to Bobby Nash for inviting me along for the ride and to Airship 27 for putting the whole thing together. Lance Star is a great character and it was a privilege to contribute a page or two to his history.

I hope you enjoyed the tale, dear reader, as well as the others in the book. Be sure to let Bobby and the Air Chief know so they can prepare the next collection of aerial adventures. Thanks for reading and keep on pulpin'!

✠

ANDREW SALMON - is a Pulp Factory Award winner and Ellis and multiple Pulp Ark and Pulp Factory Awards nominee who lives and writes in Vancouver, BC. His work has appeared in numerous magazines, including *Pro Se Presents*, *Masked Gun Mystery*, *Storyteller*, *Parsec*, *TBT* and *Thirteen Stories*. He also writes reviews for *The Comicshopper* and is creating a superhero serial novel currently running in *A Thousand Faces Magazine*.

He has published or appeared in sixteen books:

The Forty Club (which Midwest Book Reviews calls *"a good solid little tale you will definitely carry with you for the rest of your life"*), **The Dark Land**, (*"a straight out science-fiction thriller that fires on all cylinders"* - Pulp Fiction Reviews), **The Light Of Men**, which has been called *"a book of such immense significance that it is not only meant to be read, but also to be experienced... a work of grim power"* - C. Saunders, **Secret Agent X: Volume One** and **Three**, **Ghost Squad: Rise of the Black Legion** (with Ron Fortier), **Jim Anthony Super Detective Volume One**, **Sherlock Holmes Volumes One**, **Two** and **Three**, **Black Bat Mystery Volume One**, **Mars McCoy Space Ranger Volume One**, **Mystery Men (&Women) Volume Two** (w/Mark Halegua), **Moon Man Vol. One**, **The Ruby Files Vol. One** constitute his other work for Airship 27 to date. He has also appeared in **The New Adventures of Thunder Jim Wade Vol. One** from Pulp Obscura

To learn more about his work check out the Airship27 Hangar at: airship27hangar.com and the following links:

lulu.com/AndrewSalmon and lulu.com/thousand-faces.

amazon.com/Andrew-Salmon/e/B002NS5KR0/ref=sr_ntt_srch_lnk_7?qid=1328666769&sr=1-7

pulpobscura.net/#!

✠ Lance Star ✠
"Black Cloud Ace"

by
Jim Beard

His wings were on fire.

Without releasing the stick Lance swiveled his head around in the cockpit, disbelieving his own eyes. Not thirty seconds before everything was jake. Now he'd somehow flown into an immense, inky storm mass and his wings were on fire.

All around him the storm roiled, sizzled with electric energy. He'd never seen anything like it and sure as hell would never have flown into such a beast on purpose.

It was just a test flight, he reminded himself. *A simple test flight on a normal Saturday afternoon.*

But when the pilot was Lance Star, the plane an experimental one-of-a-kind jet aircraft, and the flight disapproved by his entire staff, anything, *everything*, could and probably would go wrong.

And so it did.

Through his many government contacts Lance had learned of the bitter race between the British and the Germans to develop not only a working turbojet engine, but a working turbojet *aircraft*. So, as was his customary response to a thrown gauntlet, the genius inventor decided to enter his own horse into the race.

He'd been working on his own jet theories for at least two years, but other things always seemed to get in the way. Now, with the Germans making exceptional advances and Whittle of the British running not too far behind them, Lance Star just couldn't wait for his own countrymen to get off their collective behinds and do something about it. It was up to him.

The passion to be the first, to crack this particular aerodynamic nut, was too much to ignore. *This* was what his career, his entire life's work, was all about. To surge forward, to advance the technology; to fly as fast and as true as humanly possible.

His jet, coldly designated XP-1, wasn't much to write home about in the looks department, but she had it where it counts and Lance coaxed every ounce of speed he could out of her. After weeks of testing on the ground he threw caution to the wind and wheeled her out of her hanger at Star Field on Long Island and pointed her nose to the East.

Everyone around him said it was a bad idea.

"Storm's comin' in," announced Walt Anderson, Lance's Operations

Manager for Star Field. The man bit down on his pipe and frowned, said he could feel it in his bones, 'specially in his bad leg.

"Ach, aye, he's right," concurred Kevin McDouglas, dragging a cloth over the XP-1's right wing. The Scot never met a plane he didn't like or couldn't fix blindfolded.

Lance strode forward, checking his flight gear and climbing up into the jet's cockpit. "That storm, if its even there at all, is probably far enough out that I won't even notice it. In fact…now that you've brought it up, Walt, I think I'll head out there and take a close-up look at it."

Buck Tellonger, Lance's best friend and a genuine flying ace from the Great War, looked up through the sunlight streaming down and stroked his moustache thoughtfully. From his mouth a cheap five cent cigar hung.

"Lance, I…" he began.

"Right," countered the handsome young pilot and inventor, "you'll be following me in an observation plane. Splendid idea, Buck! Always thinking!"

"Sarcasm doesn't become you," Buck threw back at him as he stalked away, shaking his head and heading for his personal Skeeter.

Once the entire show was on the road, Lance's own admittedly sour stomach began to calm down and he'd almost started enjoying himself and the XP-1. That's when he saw the storm.

Lance Star had heard the German's turbojet might exceed a speed of 375mph, the British again not too far behind, so he pushed the XP-1 towards the 400mph line. Arching up and away from Star Field he engaged the thrusters and blasted over the Hamptons, past Montauk Point and out to open sea.

Five minutes into his overwhelming feeling of success, he spotted the forbidding black clouds.

Lance's keen eyes roamed over its length; he guessed it to be miles long. Black and thick, it hung over the water spread out like an impossibly large manta ray, ominous and foreboding.

"Lance?" came a voice through his radio, crackling and sputtering. "You still there?"

It was Red Davis, the pilot's oldest friend. Red and Lance grew up together, cut their eyeteeth together on dreams of flying and working on new and better vehicles and engines. His was a voice that Lance felt better just for the hearing.

Tearing his eyes from the immense storm and glancing down at his control panel, Lance saw his dials jump and shudder, a collective dance of odd proportions.

"Lance? Lance?"

"I'm here, Red. It's just that there's this storm out here, this gigantic black *cloud* and…"

"Wonderful. I'll tell Walt he and his leg were right. Now, *turn it around and get…*"

Red's voice disappeared in an explosion of static. Lance clicked the radio switch on and off, on and off, but to no avail. He tried to call Buck in the observation plane.

"Buck, old buddy, where the hell are you, old man?"

A burst of static filled the cockpit like a million mosquitoes all talking at once.

"…am I? Lance, you…get back to…"

Lance Star called out to his friend. Nothing. He tried Red again. Same thing. Static. His dials jumped again. Thankfully, his engine seemed untouched by whatever it was he was experiencing.

Looking back up at the roiling storm he could make out minute traces of lightning skittering through its dark mass. A wave of dread, of real, palpable loathing washed over him. Precious little could dampen Lance Star's burning enthusiasm for aviation, but the tempest ahead of him had succeeded on that score.

Gripping the stick he prepared to turn. Suddenly he was in it.

In the middle of the storm.

The young pilot bolted upright in his seat, almost cracking his helmet against the cockpit canopy. One moment he was looking at the storm, the next he was enveloped by it. Impossible.

The old familiar feeling of flying into the turmoil of a nor'easter crept over him, gripped him with its niggling trill of panic. Lance wished for a split second he was in his beloved Skybolt, but realized with a cold slap of reality that only the XP-1 offered the power he'd need to pull through the tempest at hand.

The storm surged with malevolent energy, a cone of darkness seemingly narrowing around the plane. Lightning sizzled like glowing veins through charcoal outside his canopy and he eyed it warily, fighting the stick and attempting to clear his mind for a plan of action.

Heat suffused the cockpit. Bright flashes danced before his eyes. An abrupt burst of lightning lit up the immediate area with a tantalizing peek at the inner ramparts of Hell.

Another kind of light filtered into the corners of Lance's eyes. He looked once, twice.

Tongues of fire jitterbugged over his left wing. Swiveling his head so swiftly it brought a bout of dizziness, he saw the right wing matched the left. The XP-1 sported blazing arms of onrushing conflagration.

Dive!

Lance Star was a master pilot. Those around him never questioned his ability to consciously fly anything with wings and an engine and sometimes less than that. But in that jolt of doom he went on automatic. It wasn't his preferred way to fly, but instinct and a burning lust to live moved his hands and banged the gavel in the court of his mind.

Dive!

The young man pressed two fingers to his lips and brushed them across a small photo stuck in the lip at the edge of the altimeter cover. A pretty girl's sparkling green eyes looked back at him from the picture, her crisp white nurse's uniform a stark contrast to the unabashed love that shone from those eyes. A love for him. A look loaded with longing and possibility.

The storm's turbulence smashed against the XP-1 with unbridled force and the darkness of it encased him and the jet in a soulless black coffin. For a moment his only light source sprang from the dials that weakly littered his control panel.

Then absolute black.

Lance dived.

Maybe he'd lose the wings. Maybe he'd smash the experimental airplane to bits when he hit the water. Then again, maybe it'd put the fires out, too.

Lance Star didn't have the answers to all the maybes, but maybe he didn't much care. He saw a life still ahead of him filled with flying and building and loving and fighting for what was right. That drove him on. He'd made hard choices before and he'd always lived to either pat himself on the back for them or regret them. This was simply going to be another one of those times he told himself.

The Atlantic Ocean suddenly filled his view and he pulled up hard on the stick and eased the turbojet's output back. Too much thrust, too little options. He braced for impact.

He recognized rolling darkness overhead and water below and guessed he was still alive and flying.

Now Lance just had to figure out where the hell he was.

A bit of green land teased him far off to his right. *That can't be right*, he told himself. How could he have gotten that turned around?

Shelving that question for the moment, he swung the XP-1 into a wide arc. The storm still raged above him but lifting and dispersing.

Lance toggled the radio controls, holding his breath. A crackle of static filled the cockpit.

"Buck!" he called out. "Buck! Can you hear me! XP-1 to Skeeter-1 ... do you read me?"

Silence laced with static.

In a fit of anger he slammed the radio mouthpiece against the cockpit wall. Seconds passed. Lance reached out and still turning the plane in a wide arc he called out again.

"XP-1 to Star Field. XP-1 to Star Field. Red, do you read me? Repeat, this is Lance Star in XP-1. Does anybody read me out there?"

Again he was rewarded for his pains with silence. Lance hung the mouthpiece in its cradle and glanced again at the beckoning sliver of green far off in the distance.

Nantucket? Martha's Vineyard? Or could he be farther north? Or even south?

Suddenly, the radio sputtered with activity. A voice, riding the static, burst forward.

"...ance? Lance? Wh...you?"

⊬

Lance Star fumbled for the radio control, calming himself. "Red? Red, is that you, old pal? Are you okay? Did it hit bad there?"

Silence.

He flipped the switch back and forth, spoke again.

"Red? Dammit, Red, I said are you okay?"

A long gush of static issued from the radio, followed after several seconds by a voice.

"Am *I* okay?" it asked. "Are *you* okay?"

The pilot whipped the helmet and air cap from his head and ran a hand through his sandy blonde hair. A look of consternation filled his face.

"If you must know, yeah, yeah I'm okay. Damndest thing I think I've ever encountered, and you know that's me saying a mouthful. Storm's a real doozey. How bad did you get it there? Any damage? Anyone hurt?"

Again, silence. Lance was about to start chewing on the mouthpiece when Red's voice broke through.

"Lance, we're…okay here. Everything tip-top. Are you…are you bringing it back in?"

The storm rumbled just then, a long, low grumble of thunder that vibrated through the air and the XP-1. *Its last gasp*, thought Lance.

He hoped that Buck Tellonger had made it back to the field in one piece. There was still no sign of the veteran pilot. Lance assumed he made it down safely.

"I'm coming in, yep. Clear me a spot to set 'er down…and tell Buck and Walt and that damn Scot that I owe 'em all a drink…"

Looking up and straightening out his wings he pointed the jet towards the green. Wherever, whatever it was he'd have to use it to orient himself and get back to Star Field. The fuel gauge mournfully reflected the now-lengthy first flight of the XP-1.

Flying in low he found himself identifying Cape Cod below him. *Quite a stretch from the field!* He mused.

Lance also realized the sun was just beginning to set. Looking at his watch he saw that it read three o-clock in the Pee-Em.

"Dammit, *what*?" he shouted out loud.

The nose of the XP-1 lifted. Lance Star pulled the stick back and took the plane higher as he watched curious eyes glomming him from a ferry chugging back from Chappaquiddick to Falmouth.

He shook his head violently. He rubbed his eyes, glanced once again at the watch and at the sun.

"Red, what time is it?" he called into the radio. Nothing.

Fear was not a stranger to the young man nor was it a good drinking buddy. But Lance often said that a man was a fool to not accept fear as one of the prime motivating factors of the universe and just work his way through it.

He began to fight it off with every ounce of strength left in him.

"*Red*!" he bellowed and nudged the XP-1 towards Long Island. "If this is a prank of yours, I swear I'll…"

A shadow fell over him, cloaking him and the jet in a dark blanket.

Lance looked up. The shadow moved and the blistering rays of the setting sun behind it burned directly into his retinas. He yelped. The plane jerked.

Another craft swooped down from overhead and directly into his flight path. Lance gripped the stick and swore vehemently.

"What the hell?"

The other jet—he could clearly make out its turbo propulsion—waggled its wings and abruptly peeled off to the left. Lance tried to track it with his sun-damaged eyes but found it a challenge.

Finally, his vision cleared enough to make out the plane riding alongside his own. Painted in black and grey, it sported the German Iron Cross insignia.

Its pilot, goggled and sporting a black skull cap, turned his head slowly in the cockpit to look at Lance. The man nodded once, curtly, and he and his craft disappeared.

When it reappeared seconds later on Lance's tail, it opened fire on him with a hornet's swarm of hot lead.

He had no armament of his own with which to answer the question. Not a single bullet.

The XP-1 sported no guns, no weapons of any kind. It was a test model, made for speed not for fighting. *And I'm about to enter into a whole new kind of fighting*, thought Lance.

With dry certainty, the young man felt the old world slipping away and a glimpse at a new world of jet fighter battles before him. At any other time he might have been fascinated, eager to participate; being smack-dab in the middle of it with no way to shoot back held no interest for him.

Lance had gotten a good look at his visitor. Long and black, the German jet was different from his own, yet in some ways very much the same. There was a vision for design in it that he appreciated and that appealed to him on more than one level, but he'd also eyeballed areas of slap-dash workmanship and shoddy maintenance. As a professional, such things disgusted him.

He wondered where it had come from. He imagined a ship out at sea, some distance from the coast, a launching site a ship? Maybe a fleet of ships! An invasion force, even.

There was little time for doping it out. Bullets ripped at the XP-1, chewing pieces out his wings, his tail. Knowing the German ace was behind him but not being able to actually *see* him, Lance pulled back on the stick and poured on the juice.

The dark ace stayed on his tail.

Lance mulled over his options. He hadn't much considered tactics for jet dogfights, wasn't even sure it could be done at all. But preservation kept him moving and a burning desire to be hunter and not prey drove him on, desperate to throw his new friend off his back.

The radio crackled.

"Lance! Lance! This is Buck! Land, boy, land! Do not engage! Repeat, do not engage! It's the devil himself!"

Good old, Buck, he smiled to himself. *Always late to the party and always a mother hen.*

"Don't know where you've been hiding, Buck," he shouted back into the radio, "but stand back, old son, school's in session and teacher's here with a lesson!"

As he'd guessed, maneuverability would be a problem.

"Speed it is," Lance announced. "And...turning."

He banked into a sharp arc. The XP-1 shuddered, protested. The canopy creaked and groaned as a very large gorilla jumped onto his chest.

A hail of bullets all around him told Lance his black ace was still gobbling up his contrail.

"I have to head in..." came Buck's voice again. "Engine trouble...have to bring it in..."

Lance couldn't worry about Buck anymore. He put his old friend out of mind and concentrated on ushering in the art of jet fighting. *Well, one-sided jet fighting, maybe,* he told himself.

He maintained the curve, catching a glimpse of open water below him. The XP-1 produced a series of audible tics and tings, but held together. Whether he himself could hold together under the g-forces, "g" for gorilla, he wasn't too sure.

All through his admittedly short life he'd been told that pride was a sin. That it'd be the death of him. Pride of the past instilled the drive in him to become a pilot, pride of country put him on the path to building a turbojet and pride of self put him into the cockpit for an unscheduled test run; pride wasn't such a bad thing, was it?

Losing another few pieces from his wings told him that perhaps it was. He'd work on his pride the moment he got back on the ground. *If* he ever got back on the ground.

What was the mystery ace up to? What was his game? To *shoot* Lance down dead or to simply *force* him down, to land?

He didn't have the answers. He only had speed and plenty of it. He was cooking with gas and humming in the kitchen.

Lance jinked the stick and brought his plane out of the turn. *Let's see what some up-and-down Cyclone-style would be like!*

The black ace matched him move for move! Over and over again. It was damn frustrating, to say the least.

Suddenly, Star Field was ahead of Lance and then below him. He saw a plan forming in his brain.

There was a tower at Star Field. Not too unusual. It might have proved to be the young pilot's salvation.

Lance always hated that tower, said it was ugly, didn't like the paint job. Hoped to make enough some day to have it torn down, replaced by a fancy new one.

He envisioned a bit of destruction with the help of his current dancing partner.

Thumbing the button on the radio, the pilot shouted into it. "Red or anybody else, if you're in the tower, *get out now!*"

He knew the Kraut on his tail would be unfamiliar with Star Field, its layout, its buildings. That'd be to Lance's advantage.

He pointed the XP-1 directly at the tower.

"If you're listening in, my new friend, we have a custom in this country of giving a gift to a visitor…"

Static burst through so loud it hurt Lance's ears. A voice speaking German issued forth. Lance's German was not good. It stunk, in fact.

With the black jet almost kissing his tail he sped towards the tower at a hellish speed.

Before plowing into it with a split-second to spare, Lance veered off.

He waited for the explosion. None came.

Looking over his shoulder he strained his neck to see the tower intact, only wobbling a bit from the tremendous blasts of air from the two jets rocketing past it.

"Okay, this guy's good."

He hated to admit it, but there it was. Lance's mind raced to come up with another plan, though, at the minute, he's also had to admit he was coming up short.

Then he caught sight of the black ace, his contrail like a long white rope leading the eye like a line down the highway. Lance pulled up, gained some height and swung the XP-1 towards its prey. And the ace *was* the prey now.

"Betty, I need your strength," he said to the photo of the pretty nurse. "Here we go!"

He brought his plane right down behind the ace and squared its nose on the man's tail. The black craft woggled its wings a little and made quick jabs to the right and left, exactly what Lance was expecting and prepared for.

He didn't let go of the leash he now had around the ace's neck. Not for a single second. They were matched, speed for speed, ability for ability, but one of them was going to have to eventually cry "uncle" and it wasn't going to be Lance Star.

"Oh, my kingdom for a damn machine gun!" Lance growled.

They zoomed out over the Atlantic in another wide arc, then poured on the steam heading back towards land. Lance guessed they were coming up on Connecticut, somewhere in the vicinity of New London. Towns and fields and rivers sped by so quick it made him dizzy.

Dizzy...was he blacking out?

"No! No, dammit!"

Lance slammed his head against his canopy to goose his brain, creating bright pinpoints of light around his eyes. The turn was getting tighter, tighter. He couldn't imagine how the other ace was putting up with it.

"This...this guy is...is *good*!"

He hated to lose the XP-1 like this. Dreams of beating the Krauts and the Brits to the jet engine punch began to evaporate. When they wiped up the smear of melted metal and goo that used to be Lance Star and his amazing XP-1, who would know anything of what had transpired?

The photo of Betty suddenly flew off his control panel and plastered itself on his goggles.

"Okay, okay," he whispered. "Okay..."

The glass shattered on his fuel gauge, drawing his eyes to it.

Empty.

He had to land.

Lance pointed his nose towards Star Field. Towards home.

He wasn't giving up, he assured himself. He was just bowing to the whims of the universe. Fuel gauge went over into empty; he called it a day and went home. Let the black ace have all the fun, such as it was.

His head spun and he guessed he might be hallucinating. Betty was in the cockpit with him, pressing her warm body against his, breathing huskily in his ear, whispering sweet nothings.

Land. He had to *land* the plane!

Shaking off whatever was coming over him, Lance gripped the stick and hoped he had enough to make it back. He shot past New Haven and

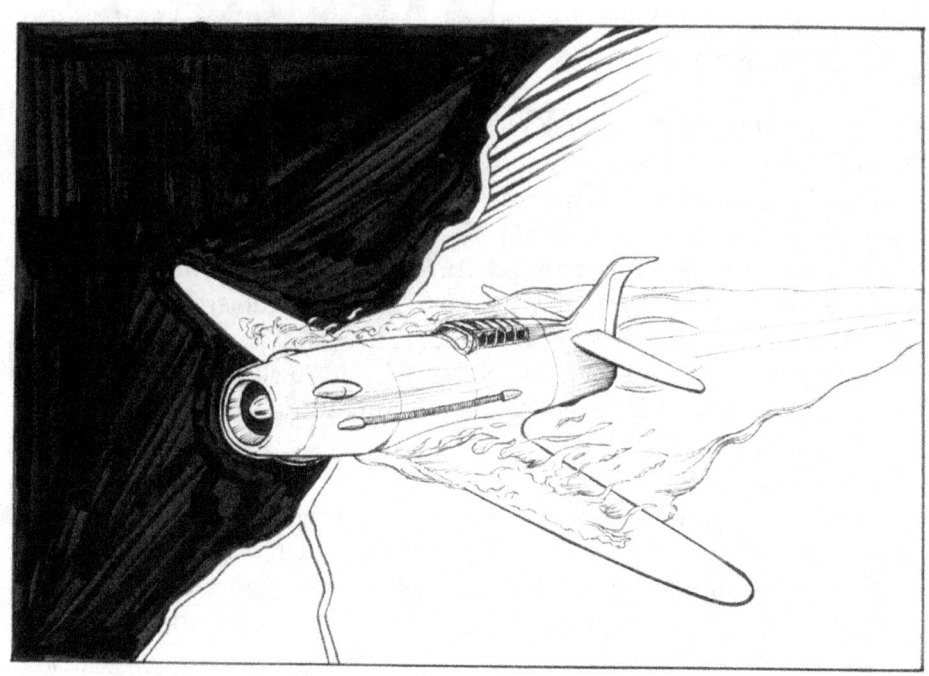

"Okay, okay," he whispered.

out over Long Island Sound and it was about then that something gave out in his turbojet and the XP-1 coughed and belched smoke.

A dirty inky trail marked his progress. He realized he was not being shot at. *Guess my friend the Kraut sees I'm done*, he thought. *All his sandbox now...*

Lance blacked out, just for a few seconds. He sat up, slapped at his face. Hard. The green of Long Island spread out below him. He looked for Star Field.

Spotting it finally, he tried to get the XP-1 into a semblance of a landing position. She fought him tooth and nail.

His mental image of the field's runways popped up for him to review in his mind's eye but faded in and out. He's put her down *somewhere* at least. Might not be a perfect landing, but he'd put her down regardless.

It rankled him to be forced down by fate. A floodgate of anger opened as he lined up with a runway, a hot tide of disgust that he aimed at everything and everybody around him. He was no longer calm, a state of mind that didn't lend itself to landing an airplane. He cursed.

He came in low, nearing the ground and pulling the lever to extend the landing gear. He was leaking a lot of smoke – maybe too much. Lance felt heat, a surfeit of it.

Crash it, a voice inside his head instructed. *Crash it and let it burn.*

It was all about choices, wasn't it? Lance Star was presented with a choice – save himself and the XP-1 by setting it down with all the skill at his command or eject and let it fall into the gaping hole of the abyss... He reckoned it wasn't much of a choice at that.

Wrestling with the stick, beating it into submission, Lance set his craft down on the runaway. His speed was a fair bit more than he was comfortable with but he touched tarmac with relative grace and applied the brakes.

Came a loud noise.

Something blew in the turbo. Lance felt heat, saw flames, felt the plane crumble. He hit the ejection button. The canopy blew and he was up, up and away.

His chute opened nicely but he barely had time to enjoy the glorious freedom of it all. The ground came up swiftly and he hit it hard, the bones in his legs and back screaming oaths at him he didn't even know existed.

He lay there for a moment, collecting himself, expecting Red or Buck or one of the others to be running out to pick him up and dust him off. No such greeting occurred. He picked himself up and dusted himself off and looked around.

The sight that appeared before his eyes was strange, unbelievable. Star Field looked deserted, shut down. And furthermore, it looked like a storm had blown through it.

An alarm went off. It took him a second or two to understand the alarm was in his head and not issuing forth from the field's klaxons.

Lance Star began to trot towards the field. Then he ran.

The fiery wreckage of the XP-1 filled the air with a black, acrid smoke, stinging Lance's eyes, making them water. He skirted the burning, twisted metal and sprinted towards the buildings on the other side of the landing strip.

The pilot guessed that the storm had made landfall, slamming Star Field and leaving the scene before him in its path. He thought to scan the sky but at first saw no sign of the immense storm clouds. Nor the black ace.

He slowed, taking in the field's offices, hangars and miscellaneous buildings. They had seen better days, he told himself. Much better days.

The men of Lance's company, the Sky Rangers, followed their boss' strict code of maintenance and upkeep religiously; the field was never in such a state.

Something's not right. This is more than storm damage, the ground's not even that wet.

He stopped abruptly, panting. Catching his breath Lance turned in place, swiveling around to absorb the panoramic view. The field *wasn't* storm-damaged.

It was in disrepair.

"What the hell…?"

"Lance! Lance?"

The young man swung around to see Buck Tellonger running towards him, across the tarmac. The older man was really pushing himself, his short legs pumping up and down, driving his bulldog of a body forward.

The first thing Lance noticed, for some reason, was the absence of a cigar hanging out of Buck's mouth.

He waved at his old friend and mentor, but kept looking all around him at the field.

In a few seconds, Buck was upon him, gripping his shoulders and staring at his face, wide-eyed. Lance thought the man might hug him.

"Yeah, crazy days we live in, huh? What do you make of it all, Buck? What happened?"

"I…I was about to ask you the same question. Are…are you okay, Lance? Are you hurt?"

Lance eyed the older man, surprised at his strident interest in his well-being. They'd been through countless scrapes together, not a few of them to the point of staring death in the face. He couldn't imagine why Buck would suddenly choose this moment to play the concerned parent.

"Went right through the heart of it," he told Buck, aiming a thumb at the sky, at the storm. "Damndest thing – my wings caught fire. Then, that other jet…

"…and now, all *this*."

The young pilot waved his hand in a wide arc, taking in the length of Star Field. Thunder rumbled in the distance, punctuating his gesture. He turned back to his mentor to find the man staring at him with wet eyes. The sight unnerved Lance.

"Let's find Red, and the others," he said, puzzled. "I need some answers."

Lance stepped past Buck and made his way across the field. The older man fell in place alongside him, slightly to the rear. He said nothing.

"Buck?"

"Yes?"

"What day is it?"

The short, stocky pilot stopped abruptly. Lance took a few more steps, wheeled around to face his companion.

"Why, it's…it's Wednesday…isn't it?"

"And the month? The year?"

Buck Tellonger rattled off the correct data. Lance's eyes bore into him, then relaxed. He blew out air, gave a weak, almost-embarrassed smile. He chuckled.

"What, Lance?" asked Buck, perplexed. "Wha…what is it?"

The younger man pushed a shaky hand through his sandy locks, shaking his head from side to side, still chuckling.

"I thought…I thought maybe I had traveled through time or something!"

Buck's moustache twitched. Finally, his confusion gave way to mirth and the two old friends shared a good laugh over the ridiculous proposition.

As their laughter died out, a black jet split the air above their heads with unholy force.

Rain began to fall, great big dollops that sizzled like water on a hot griddle as they smacked the ground around the two men. Lance wondered if perhaps he'd somehow stumbled into the first level of Hell.

The black airplane zoomed off into the distance, out over the ocean. A moment later it returned.

"He's reconnoitering," said Lance, soberly. "C'mon, Buck, let's haul out the anti-aircraft guns and give him a warm welcome!" He began running across the field once more.

Catching up to his young protégé, Buck wheezed at Lance's side. "Lance, you think that's, err, wise?"

"As wise as my Aunt Tilly's washing on Monday, Buck. Can't let any Krauts fly around like they own the place. Besides, if this is the first wave of an invasion force I want t'show them we're no pushovers…"

He had to put the older man's words, his odd actions behind him, literally and figuratively. If Lance were to function, to take command of the situation, he needed to focus on a single problem. And the black ace and his craft just won the Kewpie doll in that department, if he had anything to say about it.

Stuck on the ground while someone else ruled the skies, he saw it as a matter of professional pride. And patriotism, of course.

The tarmac surrounding them burst open in straight lines of explosive detonations. The jet had opened fire on the duo, boxing them in with bullets.

"*He's shooting at us*! Just for what I said!" cried Buck in a strained, exasperated voice.

Lance felt like pointing out the ridiculous obviousness of the statement, perhaps even the quizzical nature of it, too, but let it go. He turned his head to see his friend dive behind a small hillock at the side of the landing strip. Lance followed suit, his options extremely limited in the face of machine gun fire from an airplane circling the skies at unheard of speeds.

Where was Red? Where were Walt and Kevin and the others? He had no clew.

The sky darkened, became as black as sackcloth. They looked up to see the immense, alien cloud formation roll in and blanket the field in darkness.

Keeping their heads down Lance and Buck peered out from behind the hillock, dividing their rapt attention between storm and ace alike. There was really nowhere to go, so they planted themselves and watched.

Lightning flashed within the cloud, thunder boomed and bellowed. The black jet took one more pass and then disappeared behind a grouping of buildings. Lance noted the lack of bullets on its last fly-over.

"He's landing." It wasn't a question.

"Most likely," replied Buck, wiping the sweat from his face and touching his forehead to the grass of the hill. He looked utterly, completely spent.

Lance Star popped up from his prone position, quick as a wink. "Then let's be ready for him, eh?"

Running after the young pilot once more, the short, stout Tellonger caught up with him and grabbed at his shoulder.

"Then what, Lance?" he asked, his face painted with concern.

Lance brushed the hand away, something he'd never done before with the man he thought of as his second father.

"He's the *enemy*, Buck. What do you think?

"Now, here's my plan. I want you to skirt around the north landing strip, that's where he'll come in, I'm sure and stake out a spot on the other side. I'll mirror you on this end and we'll catch him up in the old vise-grip. Got it?"

Buck's face tightened into a pensive moue. "I...I think I better, ahh, stay with you, Lance."

The young man planted fists on hips, his patience all but eroded. "That's an order, Buck," he said quietly, the words veined with tiny bits of ice.

"We're not military, son." Something of the older man's former fire laced his own statement.

"No, no, we're not. Good point. Consider it a directive from your boss then."

The two men stared at each other, eyes locked, neither one of them backing down.

Finally, and after what seemed an eternity, the mustachioed Great War veteran nodded, shot off a terse salute and turned on his heel. Lance glared at his back for a few seconds, pondering the riot of firings he'd strike up the moment the current crisis passed.

"Just can't get good help these days," he told himself, moving once more, regretting the entire scene.

The man was practically family.

╬

The rain increased its deluge, obscuring the landscape. Lance crossed between two buildings, checking that his photo of Betty rode safely in an inner pocket and pulling his sidearm.

Clicking off the safety, he came out in the open and surveyed the situation.

The north landing strip wasn't as big as the others on the field but it was good enough for the black ace to set his jet down on. Lance squinted through the rain and watched as the dark shape of the aircraft taxied down the tarmac and came to a crawl roughly a hundred yards from his own position. He could see no sign of Buck, but trusted the man was either in place or close to it.

He wiped water from his eyes and crouched behind a stack of wooden crates at the edge of the strip. He had a little high ground; not as much as he'd like but enough to allow him to look down on his target and make his target look up.

Lance lifted his pistol and took aim down its sight.

The black jet came to a complete stop, the drone from its engine far louder than that of the XP-1. The sound eased then disappeared. After several long minutes, the cockpit canopy snapped open and slid back.

A figure inside the jet cracked his head back and forth, obviously scanning his immediate surroundings. Lance's finger touched the trigger of his pistol. It was a tempting shot, but chivalry and a damnable sense of fair play kept the young man from firing at a seemingly helpless opponent.

Let him get out of his fancy flying crate, he thought. *Let him get a glimpse of what he's facing before I blow him to Kingdom Come.*

The ace, dressed all in black and sporting a helmet and an oxygen mask, pulled himself up from his flight seat and stood. A pistol suddenly appeared in his hand. Without flinching, Lance fired.

His shot shattered the jet's canopy behind its pilot. The black ace dove like a sports diver over the far side of the cockpit and disappeared.

Lance swore like a sailor. He was a better shot than that, dammit!

Blaming the rain, he peered into the darkness, searching desperately for any sign of his new playmate. Realizing that Buck should be able to see the man from his side of the strip, he anticipated the shot that was sure to ring out at any moment.

Silence.

The young pilot swore again, took aim at the jet.

Now, he asked himself, *if that were my buggy, where would I have put the fuel tanks?*

Choices, choices; so many choices…

He sighted, lined up the shot and squeezed it off.

The resulting fireball lit up Star Field like the Fourth of July on a bender.

Burning bits of the black jet rained down with the droplets from the storm, pelting the ground and the nearby buildings with the hot slivers of someone else's dream.

Lance picked himself up from where he was pushed back and thrown down again by the blast. Dusting himself off despite the downpour, he twirled his gun on his trigger finger and blew on its still-hot barrel.

A fist sailed out of the darkness and caught him on his left temple. He saw his name etched across his vision and went back down again, hard.

Some inner instinct, some unnamed personal detection system allotted him a half-second heads-up and he rolled with the sucker-punch. Still it hurt. Hurt a lot.

The moment he came to rest against a large crate he slithered like a snake behind it, jumped to his feet, pointed his gun and fired.

The shot tore the rank insignia off the black ace's right shoulder. Dumbfounded, the man grunted and disappeared.

"You're fast," sang Lance. "Give you that, too, pal. Now come on out and let's kiss and make up…"

The sound of scuffling feet came to his ears. He looked around, found his opponent absent.

Lance eased out from behind his crate warily, senses heightened and every nerve jangling. He felt he same way he felt every time he took Betty to the local jazz cantina; discordant.

The rain began to let up, but the oppressive black cloud still hung overhead like some great sooty whale of the sky. Something told Lance to turn to his left and so he did. He put a bullet in with it, too, just for the hell of it.

"I'm not keen on a game of cat-and-mouse, friend, wouldn't even want to argue over which one of us is which. Come out and just take your lumps like a man."

Thirty or more feet away, down a long line of crates, a dark figure stepped out and into view.

Lance raised his pistol. The black ace took a step towards him, then another. Lance set his jaw, stood legs with legs spread wide to brace himself; no way in hell he was going to be knocked onto his posterior again.

The black ace continued walking forward, one step after another. Walking not running. He had not yet raised his own pistol.

Lance told himself to shoot. No shot came.

What are you doing? Shoot, dammit! Before he shoots you!

He'd have to fire himself when the current crisis had passed. He couldn't bring himself to squeeze the trigger. And he couldn't fathom why.

His enemy came closer, never hesitating, never slowing, with a confidant stride that gave dominated the moment.

Thinks he's going to intimidate me, thought Lance. *Thinks he's going to give me the heebie-jeebies…*

"Stop. Stop right there. I will shoot."

The man said something. He was close enough that Lance could see the man's jaw move, the tight line of his mouth waver, but barely open. He was speaking German.

The details of his uniform came into tight focus before the young pilot's eyes: the Iron Cross, the swastika, the rank of Captain. The cold hard lines of the Nazi oppressor.

Where the hell was Buck? He wondered.

Lance's finger tried to depress the trigger of his pistol. Sweat beaded on his brow. Like a harbinger of doom, like a great black crow swooping down low over the fields, the man approached.

The black ace spoke again.

"What…what did you say?" asked Lance, squinting through the sweat that burned in his eyes.

"I'm here, Lance."

Buck. Buck was finally there, behind him. Together they'd stop the black ace.

The dark jet pilot paused. He stood there, not ten feet in front of Lance Star, his gun hanging at his side. Up close, he could see the ace was no taller than himself.

"I said," announced the man in English, "'isn't this all very strange?'"

Dread swirled up around Lance's boots, filling them with cold, icy fingers of brackish water. He blinked, lowered his pistol.

"I know that voice…" he whispered, more to himself than anyone.

The black ace nodded, his mouth still a hard line, his lips pale and dead.

"You know it like you know yourself, Lance."

Gloved hands reached up and pulled away the ace's helmet, his flight cap and his goggles. Beneath, his face was like a block of dirty ice, carved into the semblance of a human being.

Lance blinked again. He'd recognize the face anywhere.

It was his own.

He heard a soft laugh from somewhere nearby. It took Lance a moment to realize it issued from his own mouth.

"Good, good…fantastic." He rubbed his jaw, staring at the black ace. "My hat's off to you. Surgery? No… a mask? Its good, very good, but…"

His doppelganger stepped up to him, fast as lightning, grabbed his tunic by the collar and shook him violently. A hand came up from nowhere and cracked across Lance's face, once, twice, three times.

"Get 'im, Buck," Lance croaked weakly, expecting a barrage of bullets or fisticuffs. He imagined a brouhaha like no bar or tavern within twenty miles of Star Field had ever witnessed.

"Lance," came Buck's voice, "do you still have your sidearm?"

The young pilot reflected on that, appreciated the suggestion. "You're rehired, Buck; excellent idea." He raised his pistol.

"No, Lance. No, that's not what I meant."

Though the black ace still held him fast, Lance whipped his head around to stare at his old friend. There beside Buck hovered Red Davis, looking tall and very serious. Both men pointed pistols at Lance.

"I'll need you to hand it over to me," said Buck.

"Now."

"Better just do what he says." This from the man who wore Lance's face.

The young pilot's eyes burned holes in his old friend for several moments, but he turned his pistol around and handed it over. The treachery stung like the devil.

But there's something more to this, he told himself. *It's Buck and Red but it isn't.*

Lance turned back to his double. The man stood there, trying to act casual, but he could also see an attempt to mask a blazing curiosity within him. He recognized the stance immediately for he'd adopted it many a time himself.

There was also a palpable charge of static electricity in the air between them.

"This isn't a joke," said Lance. "This is real."

"Yeah, that's about the shape of it," replied the other Lance, still pointing the revolver at his heart. "I'm real, you're real. We're all pretty damn real here.

"But the big question is what are we going to do about it?"

"The storm, right?"

"Sure," said his dark double. "The storm. I told them they were crazy, it'd never work, wasting their time. Controlling the weather? And for what?"

Lance chewed that over. Somewhere in the back corners of his brain he seemed to remember hearing about a German experiment to make storms, to control the weather. He'd written it off as hokum, the kind of junk you'd see in the story magazines at the newsstands.

Suddenly, he remembered what he'd said at the time: They were crazy. It would never work.

They were wasting their time.

"And…and that big black cloud, it…created *you*? All *this*?"

Other Lance's eyebrows went up. He chuckled, shaking his head and rubbing his jaw.

"C'mon. You're *me*. You're not that stupid. Figure it out, bright boy. I doped it out a long time ago now."

Lance looked again at Red and Buck, found them both sweating and nervous. They didn't care much for being in his double's presence, that much was certain. He couldn't imagine treating the two men badly. Oh, they'd had their share of arguments over the years and he'd pulled rank a few times, but they were his closest, dearest friends.

Someone would have to be a very cruel person to make the two men shrink as they did.

"Once I came through the storm; once *we* came through? I lost contact with Buck and Red at first. *You* didn't though, right?"

Other Lance smiled like a snake, but remained silent.

"You told them to play it cool. Until you could figure it all out..?"

It was coming to him now, quick and hot. He continued.

"And the storm, the giant black cloud, the Germans made it with… science?"

"Or with black magic," interjected his double. "Who knows with the Krauts? Some days I think they'd wire their grannies up to electrodes if they thought that would make pigs fly."

Lance looked over the man's uniform again. "But *you're* one of them. How? Better yet…*why*?"

His doppelganger stepped closer. Lance felt the hair on his head, his neck, and arms stand up. There was a distinct charge in the air that leapt back and forth between himself and the other Lance.

"I think you know," his double said quietly, portentously.

Lance stared back at him, unflinchingly. Turning again to look at Buck and Red, he found their eyes sunken and ashamed.

All at once it hit him.

"Yeah. Yeah, I think I do."

⊥

"Figurε it out, bright boy."

Several years earlier, Lance Star's cloud was silver-lined, not darkened by storms as in the present.

Practically still a kid he wormed his eager way into a small but forward-thinking aviation firm that gave him the room to really cook, so cook he did. A new innovation for an engine sprang from his mind almost immediately, like Athena from Zeus' head, and he won the accolades of his compatriots and his boss, Old Man Medevec, the "Dean of the Flying Machine."

Hand still warm from patting Lance's back, Medevec turned around and sold the brainstorm to the U.S. Army Corp, lock, stock and barrel.

Lance got nothing. They didn't even tell him about it. He stumbled upon the news while looking for a pencil in his boss' desk drawer.

To say that the young man was confused would be an understatement. Lance sidled up to Old Man Medevec and, clearing his throat and standing erect, he asked him about it.

"I don't have to explain my business decisions to you, Mr. Star," said Medevec. "Or anyone for that matter."

"But, I was going to tighten it up some, maybe show it to one of the new commercial outfits..."

The elder man frowned and folded his arms across his expansive chest. He adopted his patented superior tone.

"*Where* were you, Mr. Star, when you drew up those plans?"

"Well, right here in the offices. But, I..."

"And w*hen* did you draw up the plans, Mr. Star?"

"Just five days ago."

"Please be more specific, sir."

"While I was working? On my shift?"

"That's correct. I commend you on your excellent memory, Mr. Star."

"Now, see here!" Lance suddenly shouted. "I know where you're going with this but that's not fair! I get that I'm your employee and I was using your materials and I was on the clock, but...but..."

Medevec leaned back, puffed himself up. "Couldn't have said it any better myself, young man. I recommend you read the fine print in your contract now, the part that says that anything you create while employed by Medevec Aeronautics becomes the sole property of Medevec Aeronautics. Period."

Lance simmered on the spot, his juices beginning to bubble up inside him.

"It's not fair," he said, pointing his finger at the man. "And you know it."

His boss began to turn away, just about finished with his half of the conversation.

"Then I'd say you have a choice, Mr. Star. I will throw you a small bone…a bonus, if you'd like, of twenty dollars for your work and you can choose to accept it…"

"Or you can choose the door. There it is." He jabbed one stunted finger at the entrance to the offices.

"Two choices, huh?" Lance looked back and forth between the door and Medevec. The old man nodded, began walking away.

"No, I'd say there's a third choice."

It took them several minutes to lift Old Man Medevec up from the floor, bring him back to consciousness and fetch a beefsteak for his rapidly-swelling and darkening eye. By that time Lance Star was long gone.

"They're all the same, lad! Give 'em an inch and they'll take a blinkin' *mile!*"

Beer flowed easily and in great quantities that evening in the young man's favorite watering hole, all the better to loosen tongues and drown a few sorrows. His companions, a coterie of Great War veterans, helped to nudge his growing disdain for the government, and business owners, into a hearty hate.

As the hours wore on, so inebriated was Lance Star that he'd failed to notice the small clutch of strangers who'd drifted into the little bar and fanned out throughout its main room.

The next thing he knew there seemed to be a good ol' knuckleduster working its way through the establishment like a wave out on the sea and, dammit, he couldn't rouse himself from his stupor to join in.

Pity that, he thought. It looked like fun.

Then, silence. Or as near to silence that could be had with the roaring in one's ears that comes from quaffing ales at record speeds.

"Can you hear me, Herr Star?"

Lance jumped, startled at the voice that appeared abruptly in his ear.

He turned towards the sound, almost succeeding in throwing himself off his bar stool.

"A Ger-nan?" he slurred, brain working overtime to form a coherent thought. "Wha' you wan'? Thish…American soil…buddy…"

The man, a dark figure in a smart suit and hat, weaved in and out of Lance's perception.

"Yes, yes, that's correct, Herr Star," whispered the German. "But, you are none too fond of this, eh, 'American soil' at the moment, *ya*?"

Lance, to his credit, didn't answer. Confusion gripped him, a multitude of feelings and emotions lining up to air their grievances before the bench.

"No, do not answer just yet. That's *gut*, very, very *gut*. Listen while I talk to you. I have gone to the trouble of clearing out the, eh, riff-raff so that I may put a friendly word in your ear undisturbed."

Lance blinked, starting to become annoyed. "Get on wi' it..."

The German nodded curtly, snapped his heels together and bowed slightly. He produced a small slip of folded paper from inside his jacket, held it before Lance's eyes.

"Europe is changing again, Herr Star," he croaked. "Changing for the better. Changing into its true form; the form it will wear for all eternity. My country is leading this reform. We have need, great need, for young, eh, thinkers like you. A machine is being built, *ya*? You understand? A great machine that will help to bring about the great change.

"A machine of war."

Lance understood, despite being stinking drunk. Still he said nothing.

"Call the number on this paper if you wish to be part of the glorious days ahead."

"Why...why woul' you think I...I'd wanna *leave* my country?"

The German smiled, adjusted his jacket, his hat. "Look around you, Herr Star. Your country has deserted you. It has *slapped you in the face*! You owe it no loyalty, *mein freund*. By calling the number on that slip, you will know what loyalty means. You will come to discover what a *real* nation can do for you.

"Now, *guten nacht*."

Lance looked down at his mug of stale ale. When he looked back up the man was gone.

✚

The morning brought not only the sun, but even more confusion.

Lance found himself standing alone on a secluded spot of land out on Long Island, watching the orange ball of the sun rising in the east. He had little to no idea how he got there, save that it was a favorite haunt of his when he wanted to be alone.

For some reason, the area made him want to fly.

He turned the slip of paper over and over in his hands, contemplating its whiteness. Its existence was one of the few things he remembered from the night before; that and the words of the man who gave it to him.

What would I gain? He asked himself. *And what would I lose?*

His father had warned him of treachery when Lance got the job with Old Man Medevec, told him that the aeronautics leader coveted his ties with the U.S. Air Corp and the Army and other governmental bodies. Star Senior loved his country, but had little use for its leaders; he warned his son that the government often took more than it ever gave.

Still, Lance wanted to make his own way, discover things for himself, as was his custom. Now, he learned the truth of it in cold, concrete fashion. The School of Hard Knocks was in full session.

He wondered where the nearest phone would be.

The sun rose above the blue waters of the Atlantic, illuminating the landscape of Long Island in cheery hues. Lance thought at that moment he had never seen such a gorgeous sunrise. It warmed him, inside and out.

No, he thought. *No, this isn't the way.*

He wanted to fly. He wanted to build airplanes and fly them and become an innovator and advance man's understanding of the science of flying like the birds.

Like the American eagle.

Lance wanted to work to make his own country better, not some other nation; not a nation of aggressors. He was an American, first and foremost, and loved his country, warts and all.

A Ford pickup truck pulled up close to him as Lance watched the slip of paper with the phone number on it burn and then crumble into fine ashes. He threw the spent wooden match down and walked over to the truck.

"Feeling better?" asked Buck Tellonger. Lance saw a thermos appear in the pilot's hand.

"You have no idea."

"Old Man Medevec's going to press charges," Buck told him, pouring out a draught of hot, black coffee into a mug he pulled off his dashboard.

"Let him," said Lance, sipping at the sweet nectar of life. He smiled at the taste, at the feeling of drinking coffee on American soil. Nothing could stop him now.

Buck suddenly patted his pockets, then pulled out a Western Union telegram and handed it to the young man. "Came in last night, but I couldn't find you."

Lance read the paper silently. The older man furrowed his brow.

"Well, what's it say, boy?"

Lance gazed all around him, at the stretch of land on which he and Buck stood. He grinned like a hyena.

"Make a nice spot for an airfield, huh? Strips there and there, hangers over there, maybe a tower right about here…"

Buck snatched at the telegram, got it away from Lance and read it. His eyes widened as he absorbed the news from Lance's mother about her brother and what he'd left to his favorite nephew.

"Yep, Buck," said Lance, crossing his arms and feeling very, very tall. "I'm rich. Well, maybe not terribly rich, but rich enough to buy this land and start my own business. How do you like the sound of 'Star Field'? Got a ring to it, don't you think?"

Buck Tellonger shook his head and grinned himself. "And you'll do it, too. I know. And it's going to be a great thing. A very great thing."

Lance ground the ashes of a small slip of paper under his boot heel as he stepped towards a bright and high-flying future.

A deep, ominous roll of thunder brought him out of his reverie. Lance looked up and into his own face. He noticed it was care-worn, highlighted by dark rings under the eyes and a faint scar that ran from the right temple down to the corner of the mouth. It was a cruel face, one that he still recognized, though, beyond the years of ill-maintenance.

This is what could have been, he explained to himself. *This is a phone number on a slip of paper.*

"This is insane," he told the black ace.

"This," replied his double, "this is some kind of, I don't know, freak accident?"

Lance nodded slowly, wrestling with the science, if there was any science in it at all.

"A substitute world," he said finally. "A may-have-been. The other path."

The black ace grabbed Lance's collar and brought his face right up to his. "*You* are the 'may-have-been,' you stupid idiot! *You* are the path not taken! *I* went where I was *wanted*! Where I was appreciated!"

Lance ignored him, glanced over at Buck and Red. "The others? Where are Cy and Jim and Walt?"

Red's eyes flicked over to the dark ace, then back to Lance. "Dead."

His eyes then traveled a path back to his cruel boss. Lance noted it, told himself that they weren't *his* Cy and Jim and Walt and the rest. They were all part of the crazy world he'd fallen into.

Again he skewered Red and Buck with his eyes.

"Where's Betty?"

Interestingly, the words seemed to shock the black ace, but only for a second or two. He recovered swiftly, blinked his eyes and released his hold on Lance.

"I think," said the man, "that's something better left unsaid."

Everyone gets their moment. It may come sooner than later, but when it comes it needs to be grabbed with both hands and hung onto for dear life.

Lance Star got his moment by being patient. He didn't have to wait long, though; his doppelganger had both a short fuse and a hair trigger. Much like himself.

"The field?" he asked his dark double, forcing darker thoughts of Betty from his mind. "How can you wear that uniform and strut around here out in the open?"

The black ace laughed, barking like a seal. Lance found it annoying, but realized it wasn't too different from his own laugh.

"The occupation's been going on for *three years now*! Oh, oh, that's right, you probably don't know in your bright, cheery world…"

Lance chewed on that. "Occupation?"

Red spoke up. The sound of his voice almost startled Lance, so quietly had the shadowy version of his old friend been standing there next to him.

"The…the Germans invaded three years ago, Lance," he explained, the words issuing forth like oily bits of overcooked fish. "They hold everything up to the Mississippi. We've…"

A sharp look from the black ace cut Red off. He recovered quickly.

"Err, *the American army* has been holding the line there for about a year. From this field we, ah, we supply aircraft to the…well…to the German forces."

The man's last words trailed off; he was quite evidently embarrassed by them.

Lance swung around to stare at the *Nazi* who stood in front of him. He could no longer think of him as anything but.

"You called the number," he spat. "Joined the Krauts. You betrayed every…"

In a wink, the black ace was on him again, clutching for his throat. Static electricity crackled between them as Lance tried to hold him off.

"I became something, dear 'Lance'!" bellowed his double. "Something and someone I couldn't have become without their help!" he shoved Lance backwards violently; Red and Buck caught him.

"I was given the best tutors, the greatest heroes of the Reich to train me in their ways and customs. Perhaps you know of my mentor in that stunted little world of yours?

"His name is Baron Otto Von Blood."

The black ace could not continue. A cracking good blow from Lance Star's doubled-up fist to his jaw saw to that.

The young pilot's moment had arrived.

Lance moved. Lightning lit up the spot on which they had all been standing not three seconds before.

His shadow brother had added insult to injury by mentioning the name of the hated Von Blood, the German aviation *wunderkind* who had murdered Betty's brother in the skies over Switzerland. To have seen and heard the man's name trip over his very own tongue was too much for him to bear.

The young pilot dived for cover, certain that bullets would be ripping and nipping at his heels in an instant. In reality, what came at him arrived in the form of his own fists, laying down a brutal battery of punishing blows.

Lance swiveled and swung, landed a punch on the face that resembled his to a maddening degree. His double grunted, staggered back a few steps, shook it off and leapt back into the fray.

We're evenly matched, thought Lance. *Just like in the skies. But I doubt if he's going to run out of gas any time soon...*

"You're coming back with me to Germany, *mein freund*," hissed the black ace between punches. "Coming back as a freak to be examined and to be vivisected, no doubt!"

Hearing the guttural language spill from his own lips reminded Lance of the man who had approached him years ago in the tavern. The man who had tempted him with a new life.

"Get thee behind me, Satan!"

Lance suddenly remembered something that Kevin McDouglas had once told him during an impromptu boxing match between them.

"You're an easy mark at times, laddie," burred the Scot. "You've got an opening to your left that I could drive a lorry through..."

He jabbed with a right, brought it around in a short arc. It connected solidly to his double's left temple. The black ace went down heavily, howling like a monkey.

Lance turned and without a moment's hesitation sprinted out onto the field.

"And you look *terrible* in black!" he threw back over his shoulder.

He prayed that Buck and Red, or this topsy-turvy world's equivalents, would not come after him. Lance had never raised a fist to the two in his own world and didn't want to set a precedent, no matter how upside-down things were in his current predicament.

Rounding a corner, he pitched himself towards a hanger. Inside he found exactly what he was looking for: an airplane.

Lance's single, driving thought was to get back in the air and into the gigantic, black storm that had started the entire trip down the rabbit hole.

Looking over the open-cockpit Heinkel HE 51 that sat behind the hanger's massive doors, the young man decided it would have to do. The plane appeared to be sound and flyable despite its distasteful pedigree. Lance stared at the red band that adorned the craft's tail and spat at the swastika that sat like a tarantula in a white circle in its mid-section.

Spying a can of black paint on a nearby bench, Lance popped its lid and threw its contents at the hateful symbol, covering it completely.

A moment later and he was taxing down a runway, eyeing the clouds and affixing the photo of his pretty young nurse to the control board.

"Love you, my girl," he murmured. "Let's go home."

Under the droning wail of the Heinkel's engine, he thought he heard a cracking sound. Lance looked quickly over one shoulder, saw three figures running down the 'strip at him.

They were shooting at him.

He got the nose of the plane up and in seconds he was airborne. Below him, Lance could see his double berating his employees and then striking off in a hurry towards another hanger.

"Hang on, Betty," he said to the photo. "We're about to have company. You set out the good china and I'll see what this Kraut wagon can do."

The Heinkel HE began life as the prototype for the entire Luftwaffe, an aircraft that defied the Treaty of Versailles and put the Germans back in the air after the Great War. Lance Star had flown better, sure, but at that moment the beggar from another world knew damn well he couldn't be a chooser.

The very thought of choices chilled him to the marrow.

Checking his armament, two fixed, forward-firing machine guns, Lance poured on the jump juice and kept his wings level. He needed to find the right storm cloud and...well, he'd figure that out when the time arrived.

He circled Star Field, keeping an eye out for the black ace. He didn't have to wait long; another Heinkel, this one painted in blacks and dark grays, came up on him like the proverbial bat out of hell, practically knocking him out of the sky.

It was a move he had to admit he admired, something he might have tried himself.

Can't keep thinking like that, Lance-boy. He's just another target to be shot at and shot down. He's no kin of yours.

Lance rolled his Heinkel, scanning the airscape for his double. Dark clouds rumbled and burbled all around him, but if one of them existed as a door into summer, a way home, it wasn't exactly announcing itself.

Then, abruptly, it loomed before him. There was no mistaking it for any other cloud formation.

"Like a haystack in a pile of needles," he told Betty.

Machine gun fire burst all around him, salt-and-peppering his left wing with hot lead. The black ace lit in from above, covering Lance with a death rain. He jinked the stick instinctively and dove away. His plane obeyed but protested with a sickening groan of metal.

Lance eyeballed his wounded wing; it seemed to be holding together despite the black ace's barrage. Quickly making the decision that he'd rather be the eagle than the songbird, he leveled out at ten thousand feet and brought her around to face the music.

"Dear Lance, I am leaving you," he sang. "Here is your ring back. Love, Lance."

He opened up with his guns, drawing a bead on the black Heinkel.

Buck had once told Lance, many moons ago, that the choice between shooting and not shooting in a do-or-die situation was not a spurious one.

"Some people will tell you that shooting is the only choice," he explained. "Not true, or at least not in my experience. You always have a choice."

Young Lance grinned at that, rolled his eyes. "Yeah, I could choose to be shot down like a dog…or not. Some choice!"

"What I mean," said Buck, patiently, "is that the world is not as black and white as some would have you believe. We may only have a single second in which to make such a choice, but we always have that option, to choose. And there *are* alternatives to shooting."

In the cockpit of the alien Heinkel, Lance Star smiled to himself at the memory. *What's the choice now, Buck? This crazy world exists because of a choice. I'm choosing to get this guy off my back and get the hell out of here. Seems pretty black and white.*

Lance blinked, saw his enemy lift his nose and wings. In a heartbeat the black ace had disappeared.

He glanced up, expecting to see the tail of his opponent high above, shooting away like a comet. He realized his mistake at that moment and changed his direction to look down. There was the black plane, arcing away at top speed and into dense cloud cover.

"That's *my* trick, dammit!"

Furious, Lance put his own nose down and dove after his target. He set his hand on the firing trigger and pulled it back, firing a torrent of lead at his double. Now enveloped in the cloud formation himself, he coaxed even more speed out of the twelve-cylinder Vee engine to race to the other side and view his handiwork.

But the black ace was not there; he was, in fact, behind him.

Lance zig-zagged, pouring on the petrol and risking everything in the dangerous maneuver. His nemesis stayed on his tail like glue, his bullets inching closer and closer to Lance's wings.

Evenly matched, they could do nothing to gain the better of the other.

Lance slewed to the right in an attempt to shake his dark double off his tail. His radio spat static and a ghostly voice sprung forth from it.

"...won't work, Lance...know what you're thinking..."

The young pilot reached into himself and found an island of calm in the midst of his inner turmoil. He found, with a start, that he was strangely comfortable in the German aircraft, far more at ease then in the XP-1. He needed the sound of the propeller to be able to slip into the subconscious business of flying.

A patter of bullets brought him back to the here-and-now and he veered to the left, gaining a moment's respite from the rain of lead.

"...can hide...swastika but...more of me in you than...considered... Nazi underneath!"

Was there any truth in his doppelganger's words? Was the man really only the length of a phone number away from where he stood now?

Lance looked up to see himself pointed directly at the storm cloud, that weird product of German science and the supernatural.

He toggled his radio controls.

"You'll never know for sure, pal," he yelled. "*Auf Wiedersehen*, you crummy Kraut-lover..."

The voluminous dark matter of the monster cloud seemed to open its shadowy maw to welcome him inside. Sound ceased, as if swallowed up by the black beast. Light slipped away into its folds.

Lance Star thought of Buck, of Red and Walt, of Cy and that damn Scot; the entire pantheon of his life. *How much of it was because of the choice I made back on that beach? How many of those people did I fall in with because of who I am, who I became?*

Something buzzed in his ear like an angry hornet; he imagined it to be more bullets from the black aces' machine guns, a last volley before Lance slipped away for good.

It turned out to be his sixth sense, warning him of the worst possible scenario that could have presented itself.

Horrified, he looked to his right as the black ace sidled up next to his Heinkel, as smooth as can be, slipping into formation with him as if he belonged there.

His dark duplicate, nodded once, seemed to shrink down into his cockpit and rise again. One arm extended over his helmeted head, clutching something of tremendous portent in his gloved hand.

A German grenade.

The other Lance smiled and let go of the object.

The two were too evenly-matched. Lance repeated it in his head like a mantra.

He couldn't continue to fight himself. No man could for long, he reasoned. Hadn't Nietzsche said something once about that? Maybe he was just remembering that wrong.

Lance watched the grenade tumble end over end through the space between the dual Heinkels as if in slow-motion.

Skip Terrel, his beautiful Betty's late brother, had a theory about such moments. He jokingly called it the Time Dilation Principle, citing its entire statement as "When stuff happens, time slows down."

Time expanded, crawled to a near-halt. The grenade rotated across the gap with a kind of balletic quality, a slowed-down twirl of terror, as if tossed by some kind of demonic drum major. Lance couldn't imagine it coming anywhere near him, not thrown one-handed from one plane to another at more than twenty thousand feet. The odds were with him.

Still betting on the odds, he watched as the lethal bit of man's folly made a short arc and impacted, in slow-motion, one of Lance's wing struts.

It bounced off and exploded.

"...swallowed by the black beast."

On the ground, Red Davis and Buck Tellonger craned their necks skyward, witnessing the entire event.

They saw the two Heinkel's in what amounted to a death-grip, a mirror image in lock-step with itself. The two men saw the black ace matched move for move by the Lance Star from elsewhere.

A part of each of them thrilled to it. Perhaps they'd be freed from their infernal taskmaster forever.

Then the alien storm front reappeared and Lance's plane leapt into its embrace. The black ace followed and…

Time seemed to slow to a crawl for Red and Buck, too.

Fire woke them from their fearful lethargy. An immense fireball lit up the sky over the field, far larger than any one piece of explosives carried on either craft could produce. The sky around the mushrooming conflagration went black and the rain began to fall in bucketfuls.

A mighty, apocalyptic clap resounded through the area, as if signaling the end of the entire spectacle, the flourishing finale to the greatest fireworks display Long Island had ever seen. Lightning crashed.

Blinded momentarily, Buck and Red only dared to look again after their vision had cleared enough to risk the sight.

The skies were empty. No gigantic cloud could be seen. No Heinkels flew. It was as if the entire thing were one fleeting dream.

Both Lances were gone.

╬

A sharp snap of fingers brought him back to reality. It was a sound he'd always hated, all the way back to childhood.

Lance Star looked all around himself and found darkness, save for the soft glow from the instruments on the Heinkel's control panel. He blinked, momentarily thinking the darkness might disperse from the simple action of closing and opening his eyes.

Nighttime.

Wind whipping through his hair, he sat up straight and readjusted himself in the seat. The altimeter told him he was flying at twenty thousand feet, but little else. Lance peered over the side of the cockpit at the landscape below. There, he found "land" to be the operative word: he was far inland with no water in sight. Lights twinkled across the hills and valleys beneath him, but offered no real solace.

Where? His mind raced. *And…when? What hour is it? What day?*

The monster cloud behind him broke apart into wisps of burnt cotton candy, then faded away into nothing like a particularly bad dream.

A sense of surrealism washed over him. His compass told him he was heading west, but a quick search for landmarks provided no further clues to his whereabouts. He ran some calculations in his head, but that too proved futile; math seemed incongruous to what he'd just gone through.

Or am still going through, he told himself. *I might still be in cloud-cuckooland.*

He searched his recent memories, trotting each one out into the open and examining them for evidence of fact. The fight, the take-off, the cloud…the grenade. A flash of light, a gigantic popping noise, then…

Frustrated, Lance took hold of the stick and began turning the plane. He'd head due east and just hope for the best.

After thirty minutes in the air, he saw what he believed to be Allentown, whether free or Nazi-occupied he could not tell. The fact that no one started shooting at him told him nothing; he was, after all, flying a German plane. He was seen as either a friendly set of wings or an aircraft from a country the United States was not currently at war with.

Blessedly soon, he was over Long Island and making a beeline for Star Field, tired and cranky and dreading what he might find there.

He'd made a choice and would take his chances, no matter the consequences.

✈

A wind kicked up just as Lance got into position and began to take the Heinkel down for a landing. It kicked like an irate mule and he bumped, bumped, bumped down onto the landing strip.

Star Field was burning few lights. Just about enough for him to set down by but just barely. It wasn't the optimum conditions for landing an airplane. He fought with himself to not look at the edges of the strip for signs of whichever world he might have come down into, but instead concentrated on the task at hand.

Lance brought the Heinkel right up to the doors of one of the big hangers and killed the engine. The quiet of the night rushed in on him, along with the wind, and he suddenly felt like a piece of flotsam the tide had brought in.

Peering through the darkness, he could make out the shapes of the field all around him, monolithic and stony. There was debris, yes, but whether or not it was from the storm or from disuse and disrepair, he couldn't decide. Regardless, it looked enough like his field that he was willing to give whatever world it was the benefit of the doubt.

The wind howled, breaking the silence of the darkened area. The young man's feeling of dread crept back in for a visit.

Dammit, where the hell is everybody? He asked himself.

He began to walk down the edge of the landing strip, past the buildings and towards the main complex. He jumped at small noises, swore at larger ones.

"This is a fine how-do-you-do for a returning veteran…"

The distinct sound of the cocking of a pistol alighted on his ears.

"Perhaps then this will do."

Lance Star shrugged, deflated, resigned to his fate.

He turned to look at himself.

"When did you get here?" he asked his double.

The black ace grinned. "Oh, shortly before you did. Just enough time to stash my airplane and await the return of the prodigal son…err, sorry, pal, but no fatted calf for you tonight.

"Just a quick death."

He raised the pistol and took aim between Lance's eyes.

With an unusual air of calm spreading out through his body, Lance shook his head.

"Feeling right at home, aren't you?" he queried.

The black ace gave a small, condescending smile in answer.

Lance narrowed his eyes, ran them over his double's face, examining it.

"You…you don't know where we are either, *do* you?"

Gun never wavering from a point between his eyes, the other Lance Star frowned, giving himself away.

"Shut up."

"Why don't you just plug me and get it over with?"

"Shut *up*."

Perceiving that he might be getting somewhere but with no real clue to whether that place was a desirable one or not Lance forged ahead. If he caught a bullet for it, then dammit, he was going to have some pleasure from it.

"This has all been about choices, Lance," he told the ace. "And the results of those choices. You may choose to kill me, and believe me when I say there are days I wouldn't blame you, but I want a few answers out of you before you do."

"*Shut up!*" bleated his doppelganger. "Shut the hell up, you lousy…lousy *American!*"

"Wow, was I really that much of a schmuck?"

The black ace's eyeballs popped. "Was? You...you are me now. I mean, I am you *now*."

"No," said Lance vociferously. "You're me back *then*. A snot-nosed kid. A punk. A bully. You never grew up."

"*Shut your damn mouth, you lousy...*"

"Lance." He held up a hand, interrupted him. "Did you really make that great of a choice?"

⌐

Ii was a bold move on the chessboard. Lance ground his teeth, waiting for the bullet to slice his grey matter in twain. "Nothing ventured, nothing gained" had been one of many mottos in his career, but he silently raised it into his Top Five words-to-die-by.

The pistol in his dark double's hand slipped a little. He held it loosely now, clearly rocking on his heels from Lance's words.

Time to move in with the uppercut.

"Lance, where's Betty?"

The other man snarled, an inarticulate thing, more akin to an animal in the jungle than a seasoned pilot of the Third Reich. The fingers on his free hand curled into talons, then balled into a fist.

Lance Star's arm jabbed out, catching his double's gun hand and knocking it away. The man retained the weapon, but was unprepared for Lance's next volley.

The photo. He held up the photo like a talisman. In it Betty Terrel smiled her secret smile for the young man she loved, the young man with whom she had spoken of love but had accepted the fact that he would be away from her side more than at it, wooing her, loving her back.

And so, the photo. When the girl had gifted Lance with it she laughed at the quaintness of the gesture, the silly, romantic nature of it, but her fierce pride at managing to convey her real feelings for the young pilot through the lens and the paper welled up inside her for Lance to see and understand. Forever.

"Where's Betty?" he roared in the black ace's face, his anger seething over. "Damn you tell me!

"You made a *choice* with her! Tell me what it was!"

"I'm...I'm here, Lance. Right here."

The voice, sweet and gentle, stunned them both. The two men froze, looked at each other, looked around them.

Lance Star thanked goodness, thanked the universe, that he was back in his own world.

"No…" hissed the other Lance, wild-eyed, searching his surroundings. "You're…"

The man suddenly found himself locked in combat for his pistol. Lance had leapt on him and made a play for the weapon, grasping at his fingers, trying to pry them open.

As these things happen, the gun went off.

The bright discharge from the gun's muzzle blinded Lance. He staggered backwards with a yelp, released his opponent. Realizing he was suddenly unencumbered, the black ace made his escape into the night.

Lance swung around, stars in his eyes, but looking for his girl.

"Betty! Betty! Where are you?"

Buck Tellonger stepped out from the shadows and into the meager light. "Lance, I'm sorry. It was me. It was me."

The younger man looked up at the older man, his heart thudding in his chest. He nodded sadly, remembering his mentor's occasional fondness for mimicry, a strange talent he rarely used. He was good, very good; Lance had no idea he had added Betty Terrel to his repertoire.

"It's…its okay, Buck," he told his friend. "It's okay. Thank you."

"We just got back," explained Buck. "We had to evacuate the field, the island, really, and once the storm cleared we came back. I heard voices over this way and, well…I heard the last bits of it, about Betty, and saw him with the gun on you and…"

Lance was *back*. Back in his own world. Really, truly back. The reality of it crashed against him, threatened to uproot him.

"Got to get after him," he explained to Buck, jerking his head in the direction of his departed double.

"Who is he, Lance?" demanded the older man.

"A mistake."

They found him at the edge of the field, out onto a jumbled mass of immense rocks that bordered the ocean. Spray from the crashing waves exploded around the black ace as he seemed to search the water for something.

Lance hefted the pistol he'd taken from the other man, the feel of it both strange and familiar in his hand. He caressed the cold, blue steel and wondered.

Don't think I've ever toted one of these; a memory from him? How could that be?

He waved for Buck to hang back while he made his way up onto the rocks and began to pick his way across them. Their jagged edges poked up out of the darkness like a mine field seeded with sharp knives.

Singing came to Lance's ears, despite the booming crescendo of the ocean and the trip-hammer pounding of his own heart.

His double was singing.

The young pilot stopped, listened. It sounded to him like something from Gilbert & Sullivan. *The Pirates of Penzance*, if he wasn't mistaken. He couldn't remember ever liking that particular show. Perhaps he and his duplicate were further apart than he realized.

The black ace's jaw shot up abruptly. Cold, dark eyes took in his brother.

"Full of light, full of grace..." he murmured.

"Come back from there," Lance called to him. "You...we will treat you fairly."

The words roiled in his mouth, distasteful in their untruth. He had no real idea what they'd do with the man or if whatever they chose to do would qualify as universally "fair."

Still, he had to say *something*.

The black ace reached into his tunic and produced another pistol, albeit a smaller one. It looked nonetheless deadly than his first.

Lance stopped again. He heard a hiss behind him, then a kind of a growl. Turning to snatch a brief look over his shoulder, the sight of a clutch of people met him there.

Buck Tellonger. Red Davis. Cy Hawkins. Walt Anderson and that blessed Scot, Kevin McDouglas. The whole motley crew.

Some of them held firearms. All of them looked tense, their eyes wandering back and forth between Lance and his double, confused at what they were witness to. He thought to explain, or try to, but he had the distinct feeling that there just wasn't enough time.

The black ace stared back at what appeared to his eyes to be his own lackeys, though some of them should have been dead. If he had any doubts of into which world he'd landed they had all been washed away by the flood of images.

He studied each face in turn. Remembered each punishment, heard each caustic word, felt each savage blow.

Saw each look of concern for his brother.

Raising his pistol, he pointed it at Lance Star. A collective gasp reached his ears.

"Seems I made the wrong choice, Lance."

The muzzle of the gun kissed his temple.

"Tell Betty I'm sorry."

The crack of the discharge echoed out over the crashing waves, drowning out their symphony. The body tumbled off the rock on which it stood, hit a few more on the way down and fell into the ocean.

Lance Star stood there a moment, nodding to himself. Then he turned and walked back to the field.

The others followed, giving him his space.

"Don't you still want to know who he was?" Lance asked Buck the next morning over hot, steaming coffee that scalded their tongues and burned away the sound and the smell of the crashing ocean from the night before.

"Nope," said the man. "I suppose it's the kind of thing that's beyond me, anyway. I'll just be content that you have it all figured out and leave it at that."

Lance allowed his mentor the untruth of it; after a good night's sleep he had absolutely nothing at all figured out.

Cy Hawkins thrust his head into the reach-through from the field's little kitchen, produced two crackling skillets, each filled with what looked like mounds of sizzling scrambled eggs.

"Gentlemen," said the dark-haired Midwesterner, "you have a choice this fine morning; regular or my Chillicothe Special. What'll it be?"

Buck licked his lips, his eyes darting back and forth from skillet to skillet. When Lance got up from the table and walked to the door, both he and Cy looked after him questioningly.

"Lance?"

The young, handsome pilot glanced back over his shoulder. He looked a little older, somehow. Maybe there was a touch of gray in his hair? A wrinkle or two at the corners of his eyes? Buck and Cy couldn't be sure.

"Think I've had enough of choices for a while," he told his friends, but not unkindly. "I'll be in the radio room. Have a few calls I need to make."

"Lance," Buck said quietly. "Looks like you've got a little black rain cloud hanging over your head."

"No," replied Lance Star with a smile, "just weathering the storm, my friend. Just weathering the storm."

THE END

I LIKE TO FLY

I like to fly. Always have; probably always will.

I'm no globe-trotter and I haven't flown as much as some, but I actually look forward to the times when I have to board a big ol' jet plane and zoom off into the so-called friendly skies… I like everything about the experience, from the airports and the rush of taking off to the singular feeling of being above the clouds. Heck, in a weird sort of way I guess I even enjoy the security measures—always a few fascinating observations to make there in terms of the great sociological soup pot that it is.

When the opportunity to write a Lance Star adventure came up, I happily raised my hand and accepted the assignment. Part of the reason was to imagine myself in a small, one-seater airplane, diving through the sky and dogfighting with an enemy whose skills match my own, point by point by point. Aside from one short trip in a small helicopter years ago, I've always flown in the big boys, never in a Sopwith Camel. Wouldn't that be something, though?

The other part of my reasoning was that Lance Star, as a concept, is a winning one. This is the fourth volume of his adventures; that has to tell you something. Readers like Lance and his world and want to consume more and more of it. That makes an author sit up and take notice and want to join in on the fun—just like me. To become part of the team that guides a popular fictional character through his official paces is the kind of creative collaboration that really gets me cooking with gas and firing on all cylinders. And so it did.

One of the cool things about Lance's stories is that they're not afraid to take some chances. These aren't just tales of some mundane aviator and the boring guys he hangs around with; these are stories that go beyond the norm, and go the distance in exploring what's out there as well. I remember when I first saw the call for Lance Star stories and began to imagine the things he could discover: what could it be? Anything. Everything. The sky wasn't the limit—it was the beginning.

So, is the story of an evil twin a hoary old cliché? Yep, it is. Does that mean it should be retired? Nossir. It's a tale that goes all the way back to the very origins of civilization, maybe even before that, and is rooted so deep in our human psyches that we never seem to tire of it. Why? Because a dark side lurks in all of us…and in, thankfully, a precious few, a light side. We like these kinds of stories because they're about us.

So, Lance's "dark brother" takes the stage and matches the pilot move for move. And in the end, two universes are not enough to contain them both, so one must go. It's an ages-old story and I hope you agree with me that it was about time that Lance Star received his own version of it. Not sure if he himself is that glad for it...

Truth be told, I'm more than a little interested now in the black ace's topsy-turvy world. We only really catch a small glimpse of it, but just imagine a United States in the late 1930s half-conquered by the Nazis. What if Lance went back there? Could he help? Could he turn the tide? Or is that world a lost cause?

Food for thought. Maybe one day I'll take off and fly there and see for myself. Should be fun.

⧾

JIM BEARD - A native Toledoan, was introduced to comic books at an early age by his father, who passed on to him a love for the medium and the pulp characters who preceded it. After decades of reading, collecting and dissecting comics, Jim became a published writer when he sold a story to DC Comics in 2002. Since that time he's written official Star Wars and Ghostbusters comic stories and contributed articles and essays to several volumes of comic book history.

His recent work includes GOTHAM CITY 14 MILES, a book of essays on the 1966 Batman TV series, GOTHAM CITY 14 MILES, SGT. JANUS, SPIRIT-BREAKER, a collection of pulp ghost stories featuring an Edwardian occult detective, and CAPTAIN ACTION: RIDDLE OF THE GLOWING MEN, the first pulp prose novel based on the classic 1960s action figure.

Currently, Jim provides regular content for Marvel.com, the official Marvel Comics website, is a regular columnist for Toledo Free Press and has forthcoming comics and prose work from Bluewater, TwoMorrows, Airship 27 and Pro Se.

Please visit him at http://sgtjanus.blogspot.com and on Facebook at http://facebook.com/thebeardjimbeard

Lance Star

"Die Like a Man"

by
Sean Taylor

Lance Star opened his eyes to a stinging blackness. But it wasn't just dark, he knew that, it was thick, something putrid and burning against the soft tissue of his pupils. He tried to scream out, but no sound escaped. Instead his throat and mouth filled with the same vile thickness that hurt his eyes. He twisted his head, up, then down, from one side to the other for some clue where he was, but found only darkness in all directions.

Seawater, he realized when the salty taste oozed into his stomach. He was submerged. But where?

He fought the pain and searched for even a sliver of light to find which way was actually up.

Nothing.

He swam. Without knowing if he was pushing deeper toward death or upward to fresh air, he kicked his feet and pulled water aside with all the strength he could muster. Two feet. Five. Maybe even ten, but he feared he was no closer to the surface than before.

Should he keep going or turn around the other direction? And where was he? The last thing he remembered was testing an experimental air cannon for the Navy. He had been airborne for barely an hour over the Atlantic when …

When what? He searched his thoughts and found nothing.

One minute he was flying and the next he was waking up in black water.

Had he crashed? And if so, how deep was he for the water to be so dark? Could he even make it to the surface before what little air he had gave out and his lungs filled with the putrid water?

So he swam. Choose a direction and stick with it. Commit, damn it. At least die with a goal. Die like a man.

He thought of Betty, how she had warned him before every mission not to get himself killed. How she had reminded him with a simple kiss how much he had to live for and come back home for. How she had not thought to warn him before the kiss this time because of the routine nature of the job.

It was just test piloting a new plane, she had told him, and he could do that, and probably had at some point, in his sleep.

Of course he had agreed. He expected as some point to die on the job, but he'd always guessed that if a mission killed him it would be in the middle of the action, good guys versus bad guys, guns blazing and the

Skybolt shooting at breakneck speed through the cloud-filled blue. Over the wild blue yonder and all that.

Something bit into his neck. He reached in the blackness for whatever creature had found him. His hands grasped water and nothing else.

The something bit again.

Then it pulled.

His body twisted against the pull, but he was too weak to fight. He was jerked back in the direction from which he'd just come, and any progress toward life and breath and air was lost. Whatever the creature was, he hoped it would finish him quickly.

But rather than biting anything other than his neck, it only pulled him along. His final breaths were coming, he knew, and he could hear to his heart racing, pounding like the engine of the Skybolt, determined to find something to feed his blood and keep him alive.

I'm sorry, he thought, I'm sorry Betty and Buck and I'm sorry to all the Sky Rangers. If I had it to do over, I'd just explode over the ocean and go out in a blaze to make you and me both proud, not drowned by a fish I'm too tired to fight.

He closed his eyes, opened his mouth and let his last breath disappear.

Moments later, the thing at his neck held him in warmth. The thick, black water was gone. He cracked open his eyes.

Light. There was light. *Real* light.

He opened them fully, and then screwed them closed again. The light stung like the sea had. Only, he could get used to the light. He just needed a few minutes.

Squinting, he let his vision adjust, as he felt his body being lifted until even his feet were free of the water.

Something hard and cold hit his back and he winced, then coughed. The seawater burned as it rushed up from his lungs and gut and was vomited back into mother ocean. He coughed again and tried to speak, but was interrupted when he was bent backward and pulled under something that sheltered him from the sun.

"It's good to have you back, Señor Star," said a voice he didn't recognize. "I'd hate to lose you after going through so much effort to retrieve you in the first place."

"Where…" Lance started, but stopped when a second spew of sea water erupted from him. This time, though, lying on his back, the putrid spray had nowhere to go but back into his mouth and all over his face.

"Perhaps you'd like a moment to recover before we talk," said the voice.

"Where," he said again. "Where am I?"

"You're aboard my yacht, Señor Star."

Lance rolled from his back to his belly then pushed up to his knees. When he was upright finally, he wiped the bile from his mouth with the back of one hand.

"Domingo," the voice said, and another one Lance didn't know responded with a grunt followed by a yes, sir. "Please help our guest to his feet."

Lance's eyes at last felt adjusted to the light and he opened them fully to take in his surroundings. The man in front of him stood at least six and a half feet tall, and wore his black beard in a point that hung off his chin like something out of a Dumas novel. He wore nothing more than a pair of white trunks, against which hßis golden brown skin looked darker than its true color most likely. His arms and legs were thin, but well-muscled, and he could have been at home on an Olympic swimming or running team without seeming out of place.

His companion, Domingo, was equally tall, but thick around the shoulders, torso and hips, and wore his weight more like that of a wrestler or weightlifter. His muscles sat more pronounced on his limbs and he too would have been an Adonis, though of a different type, save for the long scars on his already blockish and misshapen face. He wore a brown suit with no coat and his sleeves rolled up past his elbows.

"It's okay," Lance said. "I can get it. I need to do this myself to get my sea legs, if you don't mind."

"Very well," the first man. "Allow me to introduce myself. I'm Rafael Alvarez, though I'm sure my name will mean nothing to you."

"Right now it means a lot, since you're the guy who just saved my bacon. What was that thing that got a hold of me down there anyway?"

Rafael cocked his head to the side and gazed away for a moment. "I'm afraid I don't understa…" He stopped himself and laughed. "I'm afraid you have the wrong idea. That was no creature that had you. That was my rope."

Lance felt his neck and found the words true. There was indeed a raw twine of hemp looped around him tightly. He tugged at the rope, following its path with his eyes along.

It ended in Domingo's hands.

"I don't understand," Lance said. "Why rescue me just so you can choke me to death?"

Rafael laughed loud and hard. "Yes, Señor Star, it's true. You genuinely don't understand." He turned and called out, "Yu."

A thin Chinese man emerged from a doorway between Lance and the confusing man who had rescued him.

The man smiled at Yu, who simply nodded.

"Have you regained your sea legs, Star?" Rafael asked.

"I want answers and I want them n…"

Lance was cut off with a blow to his stomach and he doubled over and spit up part of the sea again.

"You're in no position to make demands, you see. As for your confusion, you must understand that I didn't rescue you. It was I who had you thrown into the ocean to begin with."

"Wha…what?" Lance spattered.

Rafael grinned. "I plan to interrogate you in a little while, but first I have to make sure you understand just how serious I am about the answers I expect from you."

"Interrogate me? About what?"

Yu landed an elbow on Lance's back, sending the pilot down to his knees. While he was down, Domingo walked over, then lifted him as if he weighed little to nothing, and held him over the side rail of the yacht.

"Why are you doing this?"

"We'll get to that later, Señor Star." He nodded to Domingo. Domingo let go, and Lance hit the water as the rope tightened around his neck, forcing what little air he had swallowed on the way down out again.

"Don't slam the door again, please. I need to know if this belongs to Lance."

The bitch had slammed the door in her face, *at* her face. Only quick reflexes and the knowledge that she, in fact, deserved it and expected it had saved Monique San Diablo from a broken nose. She bit down on her anger and cracked her knuckles. One at a time.

She smoothed the front of her skirt and took a deep breath.

"Please," she forced, not liking the taste of the word. "I need your help. Lance may too."

The swung clicked and swung open. "What about Lance?"

Betty stood framed in the doorway, looking every bit the wife, regardless of her just-a-girlfriend-yet standing for the moment. Mousy brown hair brushed back and held in a ponytail. Tall and curvy, but not showing it off to her full advantage, instead trying to hide her figure in loose brown pants and a cream blouse obviously not altered to fit her specifically. Cute, Monique thought. Attractive enough in her own way, and with the potential to be almost alluring, but settling for cute.

What *did* Lance see in her?

"I need to kn…" Monique said.

Betty cut her off with a glare. "What about Lance?"

"May I come in? Or should I put the mats out in the front?"

"What?"

"The mats, so we can fight. It's a joke. But if you're determined to have this little battle between the two of us, you might want to take it inside rather than advertising it to the neighborhood."

Betty sighed. "Come in."

Monique smiled. "Thank you. I'm not your enemy. You're going to have to trust me on that."

Monique walked inside and past Betty, who reached for the door and pulled it shut. "I know who you are."

"Then you know I'm not…"

"The Saint Devil, the harlot who tried to seduce Lance in Paris? Trust me, I've heard."

Monique grinned. "So a gentleman does kiss and tell."

Betty grabbed her from behind, and Monique had to fight the urge to defend herself, thanks to the training she'd received from both the British and the Germans when she'd first signed on as an agent. Well, she reminded herself, *double* agent.

"I didn't invite you in for tea," Betty said. "What about Lance?"

"When's the last time you saw him?" Monique pulled away from the woman's grip and walked into the living room.

Nice enough, she thought, but bordering awfully close to boring. Nondescript blue sofa. Some woodwork on the end tables. A large radio in the corner playing *The Adventures of Gracie*. Only the museum-like abundance of framed photographs gave the interior any sense of character and even that said boring, mundane, undeserving of an adventurous hero like Lance Star.

But although the photographs were dull, they spoke volumes to Monique. Arranged in sets, one wall featured Betty and her brother Skip. *Dead* brother Skip thanks to his involvement in Lance's crusade, and her parents. Another section with a few that framed an older couple Monique didn't recognize from her research. Scattered throughout the room were six, she counted, of either Lance alone or Betty and Lance together.

They were kissing in the one closest to the sofa.

"Nice place," Monique lied. It was nothing like her three villas in Europe and her apartment in San Diego, which contained a more international collection of furnishings that the glitziest gallery in New York. Not to mention the array of exotic weapons that doubled as décor and, should the need arise, defense.

"Nice sofa. Daddy must do well to keep you furnished like this."

"My father is dead. Besides, you're not here to write for the society page, Monique, so you can cut the small talk."

"I'm sorry to hear that." She wasn't. She *had* known. It was her job to know. It was a button, and she had pushed. But Betty was a rock. Maybe there was more to her rival, she thought, than her home indicated. "Okay. So, when?"

"Wednesday. He and the rest of the Sky Rangers were leaving for some secret island to test a new warplane." Betty walked to the radio and turned it off.

"Still searching for Gracie's lost brother, it sounds like." Monique studied the room again, this time with strategy in mind. Two windows in the living room that could be quick escapes, if necessary. A hallway with a door that could be braced closed with a chair. A glance to the left revealed that the kitchen would be the primary trouble spot. There was no door, just a wide opening twice the width of the other doorways, and if she guessed correctly, a outside door in the kitchen that offered anyone who might be following her an easy break-in point.

"Any contact with him since?" she asked, keeping her eyes on the kitchen.

"No, but when he's on radio silence for top secret stuff, I don't usually get regular calls."

Monique nodded. Either this woman had utmost faith in Lance or she was blind to the realities of his life. Time to shock and awe, she thought, so she could see what Betty Terrel was really made of.

"Mind if I have a seat?" she asked and sat on the sofa without waiting a response, taking the corner cushion that allowed her the best view of the kitchen entrance. She crossed her legs and dropped her purse onto her lap. Then she opened her purse and reached inside.

"If that's a gun, I'd ask that you please keep it inside the purse. Or I could grab my own from the bedroom if you think I might need it."

"What will it take to convince you I'm not the enemy here?"

"You could start by not tying up my fiancé and kissing him."

Monique smiled. "I never kissed him when he was tied up."

Neither spoke. Their eyes said plenty even with the silence.

"Regardless, it's not a gun." She pulled out a rolled up pilot's cap. "Is this Lance's?"

"Where did you get that?" Betty was at Monique's side at an instant, grabbing for the cap. "Why would he send you this?"

"Because he knows he can trust me." Monique offered Betty the cap. "But he didn't send it to *me*."

"Then where did you get it?"

"First, is it his?"

Betty unrolled the cap enough to see the sweaty spot where her initials and a small heart were faded, but still visible in blue ink. "Where did you get this?"

"So it is his?"

Betty nodded and folded the cap and her hands in her lap.

"Is he… Is he okay?"

Monique motioned toward the cap. "Open it."

"Why?" Betty asked, her eyes narrowing and threatening to drip tears.

"Because I need to know the truth, that's why." Monique uncrossed her legs and sat with her knees all but touching Betty's. "Just open it, and tell me if that belongs to Lance."

"What is it?" Betty's hands trembled.

She could have played this a hundred other ways, Monique thought, but none would have told her what she needed to know. Still, it was a dirty, rotten way to treat the woman even if she was the primary obstacle between herself and Lance.

"It's best you see for yourself. Go ahead."

She watched as Betty unfolded the leather cap. Monique's gaze left the cap and leapt to Betty's eyes. They grew wide and wet. Her jaw dropped open and a gasp leaked out along with a whimpering squeak.

"It's… It's…" Betty didn't seem to be able to find the words she needed.

"I know," Monique said. "I need you to look at it good and hard. You know him better than anyone. You're the only person I trust to tell me if it's really his."

"I… I can't."

"You have to."

"But…"

"I know."

"I..."

"Please."

Betty sniffled and cleared her throat. Then she reached into the cap and pulled out the thing that Monique knew would terrify her more than just about anything she would ever see.

Betty lifted it to her eyes.

"Well."

She brought it to her face, letting it linger just beneath her nose.

"I don't know."

"Look at it really good."

"Where did you get this?"

"I intercepted it at the post office when I noticed the address."

"Where was it ...?" Betty lowered the thing to her lap, not closing her grip around it completely.

"Right here. Your place."

"Oh."

"Well?"

"I can't be sure."

"But..."

Betty coughed and wiped her eyes. Then she moved the horrible thing to her nose again. "It doesn't smell like him."

Monique heaved a heavy, relieving breath.

Betty handed the thing to Monique. "I don't want to hold it anymore."

"That's fine. Thank you."

Monique took it, and felt again the cold dead flesh of the severed human finger. It had seemed to weigh a thousand pounds when she had wrapped it in the cap. It weighed considerably less now.

Buck Tellonger rolled the severed digit between his own thumb and forefinger. The thin, pale finger in his hand seemed dwarfed by his own stout and stubby fingers, the knuckles of which were covered in tufts of graying hair.

He sat opposite Monique and Betty, a scratched and faded gray metal desk separating the space between them. A desk that could easily be used to pin him to the floor or crush his windpipe with a simple flip if he were anyone else, Monique determined.

Still, in spite of his ridiculous handlebar mustache, half a cigar dangling from his bottom lip, and coffee-stained teeth, he was a friend to Lance and the man she needed on her side if the adventurer were in some kind of trouble after all.

"You say it came with Lance's cap?" The older man wrinkled his face as he spoke.

Monique leaned forward to respond, but Betty cut her off. "Yes. It was sent to me."

"But I intercepted it," Monique said, reaching for Buck's free hand.

Buck extended it and shook hers. "Why do that?"

Betty cut her eyes toward her. "Yes. Why do that?"

Monique grinned. "It's what Lance would want me to do, of course. Suppose it had been a trap of some kind, perhaps a poison, and you had opened the box without pausing to consider precautions. Lance would no doubt want me to protect his…" She bit down on the word. "… girlfriend, wouldn't he?"

Buck rested his free hand on Betty's shoulder. "I'm afraid The Saint Devil's right. Like it or not, legal or not, she did you a favor."

Betty made a soft grunting sound that Monique realized didn't sound anything like an apology. But she let it slide.

"Let's not tell the rest of the crew about this yet. Not until we're sure."

"I'm sure, Buck," Betty said. "It's not him."

"I'm certain you are, but I'd feel better if we fingerprinted it, just the same." Buck motioned toward the door.

"Do you have a friend on the police force who can do that for us?" Monique asked.

Buck grinned and opened the door. Then he cut his eyes to Betty, who nodded and returned the grin.

"We have resources," Betty said, "that keep us from being completely reliant on the police for this kind of thing. Besides, all the Sky Rangers have their fingerprints on file for identification in case of an accident."

"I see," Monique said, following Buck and Betty from the office into the hangar. "Very wise."

"I would assume your people would have access to fingerprint technology too."

My people, Monique thought, have access to things that would make you never sleep soundly again, darling, but instead she merely nodded and said, "But my people aren't here…" She cleared her throat and added, "For the moment."

If the remark got to Betty, Monique couldn't tell. The other woman merely followed Buck through the hangar out into the bright part of the world, then entered another dark hangar. Monique stayed barely three steps behind the whole time, listening and scanning the grounds and hangar for any hint of someone following.

But other than a few friendly hellos from the other Rangers, all was quiet.

He led them to the back of the hangar, not bothering to turn on the lights, letting what little sunlight streamed in through the open bay send eerie shadows across the pavement and metal walls. They arrived at a locked wooden door that opened into a rectangular-framed single room.

He motioned for the girls to sit, then walked to a table and opened a small metal drawer.

Monique waited for Betty to sit first, which she did, dropping her exhausted body onto the wood-frame chair. Once Betty was settled, Monique slid one of the free chairs two steps away from the wall and turned it to face the door, then sat down and crossed her legs, right over left, letting the slight slit of her knee-length black skirt fall away just enough to expose her silk-covered knee.

Almost as if it were planned, someone knocked and a second later, the door swung open. A lanky red-headed beanpole of a man entered the room, and although he spoke to Buck, he eyes never seemed to leave Monique's knee.

"What's going on, Buck?"

"Hi, Red," said Betty.

"Howdy," he replied, not averting his gaze.

"Her name is Monique," Buck said. "She's a friend of Lance's."

Monique was sure she heard the muscles tighten and tense in her rival's face at the mention of the word 'friend.'

"An ally or perhaps partner, really," Monique said, rising from the chair and stepping toward the lanky Ranger. "But I'd be honored to be called a friend."

Red wiped his hands on his coveralls and smiled. "Pleased to meet you."

She took his hand and squeezed it firmly, not so strong as to give away her own strength, but with enough force to gauge the man's power and personality. If she'd learned anything, she'd learned that a good agent could circumvent hours of research and surveillance with a nice, firm handshake. Only a drink at the bar could reveal more useful information faster.

She returned his smile, flashing her teeth out of habit and letting the

"Pleased to meet you."

expression linger while she made eye contact. Men were so easy, she thought. Well, some men. And the easy ones bored her. But the ones who played hard to get… well, those intrigued her. Men like Lance Star.

"She's here on business. Remember that little adventure Lance had in Paris?"

Red nodded. "The one with that painting?"

"Monique was there with Lance."

"Oh." Red's jaw dropped a little. "She's *that* one?"

Monique turned and returned to her chair, walking slowly enough for Red to have plenty of time to line up the seams of her stockings with his eyes.

"She seems to think something's happened to Lance, Red."

Red went all business in less than the two seconds it took Monique to sit down. Maybe there was more to him than a gawk and a stare, after all, she thought. "What's wrong? I knew we should've been worried when we didn't hear back from him yesterday. I told you so."

"Slow down, Red. We don't know anything yet. It's just a suspicion at this point. We don't want to jump to any conclusions." Buck had laid out a row of cards and fingerprinting ink. While they had been talking, he had apparently finished making several cards with the print from the severed finger. He held the finger in the air about the cards. "This was sent to Betty. It's either a joke or a warning, although so far there's been no talk of a ransom."

"Let me see that!" Red shouted and stomped to the table to take the finger from Buck. He held it close to face, flipped it right and left, top to bottom and spun it around a few times before tossing it back to Buck. "It ain't his. Ain't calloused enough for a man who's been at the stick of the Skybolt like Lance has."

"I didn't think so either," Betty said, her chest heavy with a deep sigh.

"We'll know for sure in a minute," Buck said and fastened a headband across his forehead, then clipped in place a series of large magnifying lenses. He lifted the first of the cards, then examined it with several of the lenses, trading one for another over and over until he was satisfied and finally put the card down on the table. Then he repeated the action until he had checked out all the cards.

When done, he said nothing, but instead, carefully removed the lenses from the headband and put them away in a plush case, the pulled off the headband and placed it on top of the lenses and closed the case. After that, he put the case and the cards away in the metal drawer.

"Well?" asked Betty.

Buck smiled.

"It's not his. I don't know who it belongs to, but it doesn't belong to Lance."

Betty and Red sucked in a deep breath.

Monique smiled. "So wherever he is, we can assume he still has all of his fingers."

"What now?" Red asked.

"What else?" Buck stood up and as he did, the muscles of his back cracked loudly. "We fly first thing in the morning."

Lance Star noticed the stinging before the impact. That moment of confusion led him to believe he was at the mercy of bees or wasps as he groggily came to from an exhausted stupor. In his half dream, the insects grew long and thin and attacked his face with increased vigor until at last his eyes opened and in his haze he noticed the creatures were not bugs at all, but the fingers of a large hand.

He threw his arm up to block the next blow, but the force of the slap rammed into his forearm and sent him sprawling to the floor.

"I thought perhaps I had played too rough with you this morning, Señor Star." The voice cut through his fog slowly, like a butter knife through a heavy chain. But even in his semi-consciousness, Lance recognized it.

How could he not? It belonged to the man who had been torturing him for three days.

Domingo.

"I feared I had broken you for good."

Lance shook his head as he pushed up to a leaning slump. "It'll take better than you to break me, buddy."

Slap! Domingo's beefy hand sent him back to the floor.

The huge man laughed. "Good, I prefer toys that last."

"Happy to meet your expectations," Lance grunted.

The man laughed loudly. "Don't flatter yourself, Señor Star. I fully expected you to either cave in by now or be dead at my feet."

Lance sat up and crossed his legs "Indian style" for balance. After what he'd been through, dead at Domigo's feet might not be so bad. It would certainly be less painful.

But he had to hang on. For Buck. For the rest of the Sky Rangers.

For Betty. Definitely for Betty.

It didn't matter how much Rafael Alvarez's hired ape beat him or almost drowned him or burned him, he had to stay alive. Not only that, but he had to keep his damned mouth shut too. At least when Alvarez grew tired of the torture and finally began to question him.

At first, he'd been certain the rich Spaniard had been interested in the air cannon. But that didn't make sense the more the thought about it. It had apparently been Alvarez who had shot it down, and in the days since the oceanic crash, not one attempt had been made to retrieve the plane or even parts of it from the ocean's depths; at least not that he had witnessed. No doubt, judging by the little of Alvarez's yacht Lance had seen, surely a man of such means had immediate access to diving equipment. A bell? Suits equipped with Le Prieur's rebreathers? Hell, with the kind of money it looked like he was willing to waste, the man might even have the *Surcouf* on rent from the French Navy. But nothing. No apparent interest.

It just didn't add up.

Or course, he reminded himself, after the way his head had been knocked around the past few days, adding up even simple sums wasn't going to be a walk in the park.

"Listen, Domingo…"

"You can speak."

Lance wasn't sure if it was a question or permission. Regardless, he took the opening.

"I like a round or two in the ring as much as the next knucklehead, but I assume at some point, you and your boss are going to get to the point."

He suddenly felt his weight disappear as Domingo gripped him by his scraggly shirt collar and lifted him not just to his feet but a few inches above the floor.

"You're in luck, Señor Star."

"Call me Lance. I figure any two guys as close as we are should be on a first name basis."

Domingo lowered him to the floor, and Lance fought the urge to fall into a lump of flesh and rags in front of the hired muscle.

"I will admit to you, Señor Star, that of the men I have beaten before, you are one of only a few I choose to respect."

"Thank God for small favors," Lance mumbled.

"Yes, it is not much, but it is something," Domingo said.

"About that luck thing? I assume that doesn't mean you've decided to stop sending me through the Spanish Inquisition?"

Domingo started to speak, then stopped and laughed. "The Spanish Inquisition! Because Alvarez is from Spain. You Americans and your jokes. But this one is very good. I approve."

Lance nodded. He hadn't intended to make a joke. But if it kept him from getting knocked around and dunked by Alvarez and his goons again, he'd have to look into buying a monkey and renting a sidekick and taking up on the burlesque stages as a comedian.

He forced a weak smile.

"But no. Your pain is not over." The hired ape secured a vise-grip on his arm just below the shoulder. "But you will have a chance to tell us what we want to know."

"'Bout time," Lance mumbled, then caught himself. Damn, he thought. Cracks like that could get him killed, and he was sure that Domingo didn't take much to set him off.

The brute only grinned and said, "We had to make sure you knew we were serious."

"Serious as a heart attack. I get it."

"A heart attack," Domingo said as he jerked Lance forward. "But incorrect. We are as serious as a bullet in your head, Señor Star."

Lance followed as Domingo dragged him from the cell into the dark hallway, and finally up the metal steps and into the daylight of the upper deck of the ship.

The sunlight nearly knocked him down as palpably as any fist ever had. Only Domingo's grip kept him from falling back down the steps toward a concussion on the steel floor below.

"Thanks," Lance said.

"The sun is a harsh beauty to one coming from the darkness."

"Something like that."

There were people milling about the deck, but as far as Lance could tell, they were little more than spotted shadows walking around in a blur. Domingo led him through a path that cut among the shadows, and none seemed to pay much attention to either of them other than moving out of the way each time the giant Spaniard barked out the command to do so.

When they finally stopped, Lance's eyes had agreed to make vague outlines and erase the spots. The world was still a painful blur, but it was a world at least, more Monet than DaVinci admittedly, but at least it wasn't Malevich anymore. That, at least, was something.

"Welcome, Señor Star." The voice belonged to Alvarez, the face to one of the boaters at *La Grenouillère*. "It's good to see you looking..." he paused and cleared his throat, "well."

"Right," Lance said.

"Would you like a drink?"

"Water, hold the salt this time."

"Oh, no, Señor Star. As we are to be old friends soon, I insist you have a drink." He turned to the giant. "We will share a bottle of *oruzo*. And bring Lance a glass when you return."

Domingo nodded.

Lance looked for the back of a chair as much with his hands as with his eyes. "Mind if I sit down, or would you prefer to throw me overboard first for old time's sake?"

Alvarez laughed. "Not today, Lance. You don't mind if I call you Lance, do you? This Señor Star business may be polite, but it does become cumbersome."

"It's your boat. Call me what you want."

"Thank you."

"I have to say, you're the most polite thug I've ever met. You should teach lessons in etiquette to this guy I met under Paris."

"Oberstleutnant Jonas Kunze. Yes. We've met."

Lance fell into the chair. Surely he hadn't heard that correctly.

"I'm sorry. Did you just…"

"Yes. I did. I had the displeasure of making his acquaintance in Germany only a few weeks ago."

Lance couldn't respond.

"Not what you were expecting, is it?"

He shook his head, which thankfully helped to solidify the outlines and restore focus to the world. Good ol' DaVinci, he thought.

"No doubt you assumed I wanted information about your top-secret airplane." The Spaniard laughed again. "Nothing so droll. I could buy that information if I wanted it, but what I need you for is information that isn't for sale in any other market."

"Well listen, amigo," Lance said, straightening up in the chair, "I don't know what game you're playing, because the last time I saw Kunze, he went down in a tangled mess of burnt Reliant."

"I didn't say I saw him alive."

"Okay," Lance said. "You've piqued my interest. I'm all ears, Alvarez."

Alvarez smiled. "Good."

Before he could continue, Domingo returned with a large glass and a clear bottle of matching liquid that could just as well have been water.

Domingo held the bottle in the sunlight and gazed through it with a sort of admiration that bordered on worship.

After a moment, he lowered the bottle and set the glass on the table in front of Lance. Then he opened the bottle and filled Alvarez's glass first before filling Lance's half full.

"May I?" he asked.

"Of course, my friend."

The giant took a long swig from the bottle then lowered it from his lips with a loud "ah" sound. Only after waiting long enough to let the stuff swirl down his throat into his gullet did he put the top back on the bottle.

"Think of it as Russian vodka," Alvarez said as he reached for the glass in front of him, "if the Russians knew how to make a decent drink."

"Kunze?" Lance asked, leaning forward to get a whiff of the *oruzo*.

"First we drink. I owe you that for the way you've been treated."

"It's a start."

"It's most improper business, this torture, Lance, but you see, a man in my position can't afford to have people think him soft. You simply had to know that I…"

"That you meant business. Yeah, I've heard it a few times." Lance lifted the glass. "Just for the record, I'm clear on that. You mean business. I get it. No need to drown me again or break out the torches."

Alvarez laughed. "You intrigue me, Lance. No wonder she finds you so fascinating."

"She?"

"The Saint Devil, of course."

"Monique San Diablo. I should have known she'd be mixed up in anything like this."

Alvarez lifted his glass between them. "More talk shortly, but first we drink." He tinked his glass against Lance's. "To beautiful women and the death of our enemies!" he shouted into the sea air. He downed the top third of his glass and slammed it down on the table as though he had defeated the drink.

Lance nodded and took a long, hard swig of the stuff himself, only to cough and sputter, then spew most of what he'd swallowed back onto the table.

Alvarez and Domingo burst into howling laughter.

Lance steadied his stomach for a second drink, and instead of tossing a huge swallow down his throat at once, he held the glass to his lips long enough to let a steady stream of the stout liquid roll down his esophagus and into his gut. His eyes felt like they wanted to burst into either tears or flame or both, and his stomach muscles threatened to constrict, but he held command over his body and calmly set the glass on the wet tabletop after a few more seconds than he would have preferred.

"Much smoother the second time around," he said, but couldn't prevent a single cough from escaping. "Pardon me."

His hosts laughed again, but not as loudly this time.

"Well done, Lance Star."

"Now, about this business with Kunze and Monique."

"Monique, is it?" Alvarez grinned. "I see."

"Not for lack of trying, you don't. Nothing like *that* happened. Not with me."

Alvarez stared at him intently for a moment, then nodded and glanced to Domingo and back again. "I see. Then you are less a man than you could be, I assure you." He drained another huge swallow of *oruzo*, gulped, and slapped the glass down again. "It is a night to never forget, a night with that wildcat."

"Whatever." Lance pushed the remainder of his drink away. "I drank. Let's talk."

Alvarez's smile fell flat. "If you wish. But when we are done, you may wish you had taken more time to enjoy your drink."

"I'm waiting."

"No matter. We shall talk." Alvarez turned to his goateed hired goon. "Bring me the map, the scorpions, and the knives." Then back to Lance. "Shall we get, as you Americans say, down to business?"

"Are you sure this is the right place?" Monique asked as she stared out the window of a Rangers cargo plane. Her back still argued with her about the sanity of spending the night in a cot at Star Field, but the offer to bunk up with Betty just hadn't been her idea of fun either. "This seems like the middle of nowhere."

"Where better to do top-secret testing?" Betty replied.

"Of course."

"Are these two gonna go at the whole time?" Red asked.

If even the Ranger were picking up on the sarcasm between them, then Monique was certain that her constant comments were getting on Betty's last nerve, which was of course, just want she wanted.

Betty sat in the co-pilot seat next to Buck, and Monique found herself relegated to the back of the plane with the younger man. Though he was Lance's equal in age and one hell of a mechanic, not to mention one of Star's oldest friends, compared to Lance's adventurous spirit and air of worldliness, Red seemed to her little more than a trainee on his first mission. But if Lance trusted him, then she guessed she could too.

Thanks to the seating arrangements, she could only see the back of Buck's and Betty's heads, and couldn't read their eyes to get the kind of information she kept fishing for throughout the flight, but even working with that disadvantage, she could only keep throwing the bait out and see what she hooked.

"Is this somewhere Lance tests his planes often?"

"Not usually," Red chimed in. "Usually he's out at…"

"Someplace you'd know about if he trusted you," said Betty. "And Red, don't let her curves fool you. Even snakes have those when they slink around in the garden."

"She's only here to help."

"No, Betty's right," Monique said. "I wouldn't trust me as far as I could throw me. This could all be a ruse to steal your secrets and whisk Lance away to my secret island and make him my husband."

Red laughed, then stopped and stared at her. She smiled, then grinned, then laughed herself.

"Of course I'm kidding, Red. I have no interest in being tied down with, or for, just one man." She waited for him to laugh again. "But I still wouldn't trust me. After all, I'm sure Lance has told you all about me."

"Oh yeah."

"A shame he didn't mention much about Betty to me during our time together."

"As I recall, he was running for his life and trying to save yours as well at the time," Betty chimed in.

Good, Monique thought, resting her hand on the scar beneath her pants leg, the scar where a rat had started to make a meal of her leg while Lance was equally a hostage beneath Paris during their first "mission" together. She pushed the memory aside and focused on the bite in Betty's words instead. She could almost physically feel the anger in those words. A few ruffled feathers might help keep the civilian woman alive should worst come to worst.

"Of course, dear. I didn't mean to imply that he didn't think about you, only that I wish I knew more about you myself."

"Right."

"Here we are," Buck interrupted.

"'Bout damn time," Red said. "I'm getting antsy back here."

Though she agreed with the thought, Monique decided not to voice it. Instead, she smiled at Red and said, "Is my company that boring, Mr. Davis?"

He cleared his throat and looked up then at the floor of the plane, anywhere but at her, she noticed. "I didn't... I mean, that's not what I..."

"It's okay, Mr. Davis. I'm only pulling your leg."

Betty sighed loudly from the cockpit. The sound made a hiss over the comms.

"Careful, Red," she added, "I think this tiger may be a little out of your weight class."

Monique tapped Red's shoulder and gave him her warmest smile. "I'm just a pussy cat, really." She placed her hands on his knee. "A girl can't be too careful in this mean ol' world, now, can she?"

Red returned the smile. "Thank God we're here," he said, looking out a window. Monique did the same, physically moving him to get a better view. He grunted softly, then cut his eyes at her with a *Hey, Lady, what gives?* look she could make out easily by the narrowing gaze, then relaxed his face and body and gave up the space at the window.

She almost said thanks, then caught herself. She wasn't here to make friends, after all. She was here to find Lance. Particularly since any trouble he might be in would most likely be her fault. And if being a bitch was the only way to keep Lance's "family" away from her and safely out of harm's way, then so be it. The last thing she needed on her conscience was a dead Betty.

At least not unless she went to the great beyond thanks to natural causes, of course.

"I don't see anything," she said.

"Didn't expect to," Buck replied.

"If Lance did go down, his life raft would have floated miles away by now, or..."

"Or he'd be at the bottom of the sea," Monique whispered.

Red shook his head. "Never. Not Lance."

"I'm sure you're right. Monique strained her eyes to take in every detail of the water below. "How low can you get us, Mr. Tellonger? Close enough to make out the currents?"

"I can all but kiss the salt out the waves, Ms. San Diablo, if I have to, for all the good it will do us. He could be anywhere, and the waves could have taken him in any number of directions in the past few days."

"Besides," Betty added, "if he were missing, the government would have already contacted Buck about helping to look for him." She paused. "Red?"

Before Monique could even question what was going on, she felt something press into her back. Something remarkably like a pistol.

"And here I thought we were all friends, Red."

"Lance is my friend, ma'am. Your status is still up in the air. I may not be the worldliest man in the Sky Rangers, but I'm not going to fall apart the first time a pretty girl gives me a smile."

She laughed. "Up in the air. Very funny, Mr. Davis."

"Unintentional, but thanks. Now why don't you turn around and have a seat so we can all get up to date on just what game you're trying play here."

Monique stepped away from the window, gauging the distance between her and Red. Close enough to disarm him, but not without risking a stray shot, and that wouldn't do. Too many targets in too tight a space.

Instead she turned away from the window and sat down in front of him. She glanced down the length of her left leg, and when he followed suit and watched it too, she struck with the right and kicked the gun from his hand without risking even a single shot. The left then danced across the air of the cargo hold and her heel connected with Red's jaw, sending him reeling into the metal floor.

But the mechanic was fast, much faster than she had anticipated, and as she dived for the fallen pistol, he was also already on his way toward it as well. Her boot heel found his back and slowed him down a second or two, but the gun was still a good foot and a half out of reach.

She raised her foot to kick Red again but his lanky grip encircled her ankle and pinned her boot safely away from his face and body.

She grinned, quickly realizing his rookie mistake. He was one hand short now, and the pistol was as good as hers.

One last push against the floor of the plane with her free leg, and she tightened her slender fingers around the hand grip.

Monique whipped the pistol around as she turned on her shoulders and brought the muzzle to rest a few inches from Red's temples. "I appreciate a boy who plays rough as much as the next girl, Mr. Davis, but I'd rather you let go of my ankle now, please."

"Not so fast, Saint Devil."

Betty's voice.

Monique glanced toward the front of the plane, only to find that

Lance's fiancée no longer occupied the co-pilot seat. Instead, her angry form straddle Red, a dark bookends on each side of his waist, and an American Winchester rifle made a line from her shoulder to a perfect kill shot at Monique's heart.

"You wouldn't fire that in here, Betty."

Betty stepped closer, her boots at Red's shoulders now.

"Try me."

Monique studied her opponent's eyes. Lance had chosen well. She actually felt a tinge of jealousy for the first time in a very, very long time.

"You okay, Betty?" Buck asked.

"I'm good," she answered, then prodded Monique with her boot. "Drop the pistol, then get up."

"Whatever you say, Ms. Terrell. We're all friends here."

She handed the pistol to Red, who shoved it into a holster at his side, then she pushed up to her knees.

"Right. And I'm the Easter Bunny."

"Cute," Monique said.

"That's far enough."

"You're the boss."

"Lean over, face on the floor, hands behind your back."

"Really? Is this necessary?"

"I'd listen to the lady, ma'am," Buck interjected. "Even Lance says she's got an itchy trigger finger when she's upset."

"And you've got a way of making me very upset, Ms. San Diablo."

"It's a gift," Monique said, complying with the demand.

"Red, tie her wrists."

"Gladly."

"You seem like you've done this to a woman before, Mr. Davis."

"I'm sure I don't know what you mean, ma'am."

"I'm sure," she said, as he tightened a rope around her wrists. "A little tighter, please. Makes me feel like Evalyn Knapp."

"Pauline?" Red asked.

"Sure. I hear she liked it as much as I do."

"Don't listen to her, Red. She's just trying to get under your skin."

Red finished his knots, and helped her up to the flat, metal bench that ran the interior length of the hold. She wriggled in the bindings, found them adequate, but far from perfect, and nodded.

"Not bad, Mr. Davis, but I know some Germans who could give you a few pointers." She grinned. "If they weren't dead, of course."

"Drop the pistol and get up."

Betty took a seat beside her. "Enough."

"Like I said, you're the boss."

"Now tell me about this finger. You didn't really expect us to fall for that, did you?"

Monique crossed her legs. "Well, I had hoped you would. It would have made this trip a lot easier."

"What do you want with Lance? Why are you trying to track him down?"

Before she could answer, Red interrupted. "Who's paying you to find him?"

She laughed. "Nobody's paying me, Mr. Davis. Believe it or not, I'm the good guy here."

"And I'm still the Easter Bunny."

"Then quietly hop away while I talk sense with the grown-ups please, young lady." She waited for a retort, and Betty didn't disappoint.

"I say we drop her right here and let the sharks and waves take care of her."

"There's hope for you yet, Betty."

Betty glared at her, then looked away. "Just… just shut up."

"Okay, listen." Monique sat flatly. "We've gotten off on the wrong foot here. Sure, I tried to fool you, but only because I care about Lance and I think he's in real trouble. I told you, I'm the good guy here."

"If Lance were in trouble, I'd know about it." Betty turned again to face her. "We'd all know."

"Then you are severely underestimating the people I suspect, people who wouldn't waste a second thought about hurting your boyfriend in order to get to me."

"They can have you as far as I'm concerned."

"I'm sure, but would Lance feel that way?"

Betty stopped short, her face suddenly tight and drawn down in deep thought. After a few moments, she relaxed and sighed loudly. "Damn it."

Monique laughed. "He's a better man than either of us give him credit."

"So talk."

"How 'bout a little show of good faith with the rope?"

"I don't think so."

"It's okay," Monique said with quick toss of her head to move the hair out of her eyes. "Give me another minute or two and I'll be free anyway."

"Hey, Buck," Betty called out.

"Yeah?"

"Go ahead and head out to the real spot. I don't trust her completely, but I'm not willing to risk Lance's health on that."

Buck laughed out loud. "I changed course three minutes ago." He shoved a cheap cigar in his mouth and lit it, then inhaled and exhaled, filling the cabin with stinky, course smoke. "Now you two make nice and shoot straight. We'll be there before dark."

"I told you nothing happened," Lance cried as the Spanish blade drew a rivulet of red from his elbow to his wrist. "I have a girl…"

"And I told you that I don't believe you. I have a wife in Barcelona, but alas, we men of the world, we cannot be held down by one woman, can we?"

"Then I'm a better man than you a…aaaarrrrgh!"

The knife retraced the line of blood, this time a fraction of an inch deeper.

"I suppose you would like to make friends with the scorpions again, Lance."

"I…. told… you… the truth."

Alvarez dropped his shoulders and sighed. Then he turned to Domingo. "I like this one. He is full of the *machismo*. My grandfather would drink to his honor, God bless the old saint."

"He has a high threshold of pain."

"It's more than that, Domingo. I'm beginning to believe him. While I'm not convinced it makes him a better man, I do believe our guest probably did not enjoy the passions of the Saint Devil."

"Couldn't we have decided that an hour ago?" Lance asked weakly.

"Sadly, no." Alvarez stood up and walked to the edge of the boat. "Ah, I see we are approaching our home, Domingo. Please ready the ship for docking, and I will continue with our guest."

Domingo gathered the blades into his arms, leaving Lance bleeding over an empty table. Then he bowed to excuse himself before disappearing into bowels of the boat.

"Why…" Lance glanced around the splatter pattern that decorated the top of the table. "Why all this? What is it you actually want to know from me?"

"Well, to be honest, I now know the first thing I wanted to learn. After all, a man needs to know the mettle of his competition for the heart of a woman, especially when the woman in question is as much an enemy as a wild creature to be tamed."

"You tortured me to find out if I'd slept with Monique?" Lance felt the anger give him volume that he hoped made him seem more in control of his exhausted body.

Alvarez smiled.

"Now, to the remaining business as hand, my friend."

Right, Lance thought. My friend. Right.

"There is the simple matter of some missing paintings."

"What paintings?"

"Don't play games with me, Lance. I'm not sure how much longer you could enjoy my games."

"Look, Alvarez, I honestly have no idea what you're talking about. I've only had one run-in with Ms. San Diablo, and the only paintings involved were fakes."

Alvarez raised a single eyebrow.

"A ruse to draw out the Germans."

The Spaniard shook his head.

Lance closed his eyes. "No?"

Alvarez nodded.

"You're kidding me? So the real ones never made it back?"

Alvarez returned to the table and rested his hands on Lance's shoulders. "The originals were never at the Louvre, my friend. They were in my private gallery, and Monique borrowed them from me to have an authentic copy made for her ruse."

"You?"

"Yes. Me."

"So…"

"Our friend can be, shall we say, rather convincing." Alvarez tightened his fingers on the bare meaty pulp of Lance's shoulders. "Alas, my originals never made it back to me. Only another set of fakes."

"So she not only conned the Nazis, but she managed to steal your already stolen art out of from under you." Lance refused to let his inflection go up and turn the statement into a question."

"A personal mistake I intend to rectify…" He dug his fingers into the fresh bruises on Lance's neck. "With your help, of course."

"Fat chance. I'm not saying I agree with her in any shape or fashion, but I'm not going to give her over to the likes of you, even if I did have a clue where she took the paintings, which, as I said, I don't."

Fingers clenched the tender skin of his bruises again, and Lance winced but didn't cry out.

"I'm sure I can convince you to reconsider, my friend."

Lance glanced back over his shoulder and locked his eyes with those of his host. He forced a smile, but thought better of arguing the point.

"But let's give it a rest, shall we, as you Americans say. Instead, let's take in the view of my home as we approach. There's nothing quite like the view of a man's home when he returns to his kingdom."

Lance didn't ask if that was supposed to be literal or figurative. He guessed he'd learn that soon enough.

Alvarez helped him stand, then walked him over to the railing. The sunlight hit him direct without the canopy to protect him, and his eyes shut down for a moment, then turned off completely. After spotting up the darkness in front of him before focusing into something remotely resembling reality, he squinted and made out the expanse of an island in front of him, lush and green and floating all by its lonesome in the big blue ocean.

Both watched without speaking as the boat approached, though not in the silence that cheap paperbacks would have described. Instead they listened to the arrangement of the sounds, layer on layer, the waves listing against and under the seagull's caws, and the low hum of the boat's engine thrumming its constant rhythm. Every now and again the wind would cut through the deck and tinkle the chimes hanging above the table.

As they got closer, Lance noticed that the green didn't come from trees, but from a thick covering of grass and bushes, creating a sort of knee-high carpet of foliage that disappeared directly into the sea. No trace of a beach or dock anywhere in sight.

When they got closer, he figured it was time to bring up that point before they wrecked the boat.

But his host only laughed and pointed at a clearing off to the left where the bushes separated and a river only a few feet wider than the boat flowed into what he could only guess was the interior of the island.

"My driveway," Alvarez bragged. "You like?"

"It's the most beautiful prison I've ever seen."

Alvarez waved his arm across the expanse of the island as it lay before them. "It's no prison, Señor Star. This is *Il Sogno Più Bello*."

"The Beautiful Dream," Lance said.

"The *Most* Beautiful Dream," Alvarez corrected him.

"Named it yourself, I guess."

Alvarez shook his head. "Alas, no. But it fits, does it not? And wait until you see the gardens inside. The island was named by Italian adventurers who made it their home until English pirates discovered the island in 1854 and murdered the residents and claimed it as a place to hoard their treasures."

"A history of violence. I would have guessed as much."

Alvarez smacked him hard on his back and spat out a loud, full belly laugh. "You Americans and your sense of drama."

The boat pushed on into the mouth of the narrow river, where it soon became boxed in between two high rock walls that gave even Lance a sense of claustrophobia. The rocks seemed to him a fist that could tighten its grip at any moment and crush the vessel to shattered pieces.

"Domingo says this part of the trip feels like a coffin," Alvarez said.

Lance nodded. Domingo knew what he was talking.

The coffin walls continued for several minutes as the boat floated up the river into the island's interior, and occasionally Lance would see a lizard skitter along the rocky surface, but for the most part the coffin lived up to its name and held few living creatures within its serpentine path. Eventually, however, the cliffs stopped and the passageway opened into a lake surrounded by a lush garden of greens, dotted with a rainbow of flowering trees and ground cover.

"*La resurrección!*" Alvarez exclaimed as the walls fell away behind them.

Lance couldn't help but agree.

Within the garden, the "death" of the coffin seemed to give way to life, all kinds of life. The trees were a playground for a melee of gibbons that chased one another from branch to branch. Birds hit the sky like a cannon shot of color. Both were far too exotic for the Atlantic, but no doubt Alvarez was the type to collect rare wildlife as eagerly as art and people.

"You're a confusing man, Mr. Alvarez," Lance said at last.

The Spaniard laughed loudly.

"I mean, one the one hand, you obviously don't have an ounce of old-fashioned morality in your body."

"Yes," he said, "The American Golden Rule."

"A little older than America."

Alvarez nodded.

"But on the other hand, you seem to have a vast appreciation for the good and beautiful."

"I can't argue with that, my friend."

"But I've got a feeling you never will learn to enjoy it."

"How so?" Alvarez's brow furrowed, and the expression brought Lance a great deal of happiness.

Lance looked up to follow a sudden burst of blue and yellow birds from the garden's floor. As his did, he both heard and felt the bones of his neck pop loudly.

"Because for you, I get the feeling it's just another thing to own."

Without looking at his host, Lance continued. "Just like you want to own Monique and tame her. I believe 'tame' was the word you used, right?"

"Touché. Perhaps you are correct."

As the boat pushed on to the dock on the opposite side of the lake, Lance noticed a dirt road leading into the forest toward the North. A single motorcycle lay against a tree at the mouth of the road.

"Where's that lead?" he asked.

"Ah, you have quite the nose for aircraft, my friend." Alvarez slapped him on the back again, re-igniting the pain from the bruises and cuts. "That little nightmare of a road leads to my private airstrip. I am too rich a man to be satisfied with only boats."

Lance watched as a trio of the apes all but marched to the beach to welcome them.

"Perhaps, once this nasty business is behind us, and my art has been returned to me, I will show you some of my prized airships."

Lance nodded, already formulating a plan.

The blue ocean had turned to black nearly an hour ago, along with the sky, not that it hurt. Monique stared out the open cargo door, puncturing the darkness with a searchlight, but hadn't found a single piece of wreckage to indicate where Lance's experimental air cannon might have gone down.

"I don't get it," Betty said, walking up behind her. "According to the information from the Navy, this is where they lost Lance's signal."

Monique turned to Betty and almost touched the younger woman's shoulder to comfort her. Almost. "We'll find him."

"We might have found him already if not for your cut-off finger nonsense."

Monique returned her gaze to the sea. The winds whipped the surface into a living blanket of water.

"Well, to be fair, I didn't want you involved in the first place. You were only supposed to get me to the Rangers so they'd trust me and tell me where to find him. I'm sure Lance won't be happy with me dragging a civilian into this mess, especially you."

"Still at it," Red said.

"Focus, ladies," Buck barked from the pilot's seat.

"So," Betty began after a loud sigh. "What we're supposed to believe is that you intercepted a message from the SIS about an American warplane going down and you immediately thought of Lance and ran to his rescue?"

"No." Monique was already way past tired of explaining it over and over again. "I received a wire from my superiors at the SIS about the *possibility* of an American warplane crashing in the ocean. They intercepted it from your Navy, who apparently didn't feel like getting in a hurry to let you know."

"And you suspect the Nazis of gunning him down to study the new plane?"

"That's what the Navy suspects. What I suspect is far worse."

"Worse than the Nazis?"

Monique laughed softly. "Your innocence is so charming, Betty. That must be what Lance loves about you."

"Spill it, sister."

"Sure. If I'm right, I'm afraid Lance's troubles have nothing to do with the plane at all." He voice dropped to little more than a whisper. "If I'm right, it's all my fault."

"What?!"

"Good news, ladies!" Buck yelled from the front.

"Yeah?" Monique asked.

"What's that?" Betty asked.

Buck's voice, Monique noticed, had increased in pitch and tempo, so either he was a fantastic actor or his excitement was genuine. She kept the light moving on the water below but she partitioned her attention to the older man's words.

"Well, that tracking relay Lance convinced me to install in the air cannon... let's just say it was a good idea. I just got a signal."

"Where?" Monique turned to gage Betty's expression, but Ms. Terrell was already on her way to the cockpit.

"It's faint, but it's trackable."

"Where is it, Buck?" Betty asked, her voice weak, but loud. Monique felt certain she was fighting tears.

"About six miles northeast. I'm already changing course."

✦

Lance Star dove. It was as simple as that. No languishing thought process. No deliberation at all. He just climbed the railing, pointed his body at the salty water, and shot like a arrow into the lake.

He waited for the bullets, digging with both hands to put as much water between himself and the boat as possible. As bad as things had been, if he failed and was recaptured, he knew they would be worse. Far worse.

At last a sequence of lead riveted the surface of the water, but they stopped far short of him. Good old physics, he thought.

And he swam.

Damn, did he swim.

Moments felt like minutes, and those same minutes lingered into what felt like hours, but he dared not stop paddling and kicking. The air in his lungs gave out, and he longed to surface and take a breath, but no, he couldn't risk it. Here below, down here the bullets couldn't touch him, and up there, well, one good shot and even if Domingo and the rest of the crew didn't aim for a kill...

Not a risk he could take.

He pressed on, fighting his burning lungs and the salt that stung his eyes.

Moments more, and his hands grabbed dirt.

The beach!

He pushed his head above water, grabbed a quick breath, then ducked below again, waiting for the shot that didn't come.

Again he surfaced.

Turned.

The boat wasn't much further than where it had been when he jumped. No one else appeared to be in the water with him. Alvarez was yelling at his crew to put the guns away, that he needed Lance alive, you good for nothing idiots. Think, *Dios mio*, think!

He stepped from the water onto the sand. His eyes scanned the edge of the forest, finally locking onto the dirt road Alvarez had said headed to the airfield.

He was an airman, and if he could only reach a plane, Alvarez would get what was coming to him. All other thoughts vanished, and he let him mind focus on that one, single, driving goal; reach a plane, any plane, before Alvarez's men caught him.

His feet braced for the sprint to come.

Forget about the pain in your legs. Forget about the scorpion stings. Forget about the burns and the cuts and every god-forsaken, evil thing that bastard has done to you.

He moved like one of the bullets from his own Skybolt.

Forget about Betty and Buck and Monique and worry about them later.

Just get to that airfield and plant yourself in the cockpit of something that could get you airborne and miles away over the ocean.

He spared a moment, but no more, to glance back toward the ship. It approached the dock, but still had about twenty or so feet before anyone could disembark.

Turning back to the road, he ran.

When he reached the mouth of the road, he heard voices from the boat. Yelling for him, he assumed, but he didn't give them the time to try to understand. About a hundred feet ahead, the road curved to the right, and he hoped that was the entry to the airfield.

The voices grew quiet.

The silence frightened him more than the sound.

In another minute he made the curve in the road.

His heart sank.

The road snaked into another curve, this time to the left, and beyond that he dared not think.

He pressed on.

The left lead into another right, and he heard the sound of a motor far behind him.

No time left to stick to the road, he realized, and he entered the thick green and brown of the forest for cover.

In moments a jeep passed by and he waited, listening for it to stop. Barely fifteen seconds later, it did, and the engine turned off.

Lance smiled.

He was almost at the airstrip after all.

Up ahead, Alvarez shouted instructions to his men in Spanish that rattled off so fast Lance couldn't make it out. He inched carefully toward the sound and after a few minutes, he stood behind a patch of dense brush as the edge of the forest looking out onto a single dirt strip that ran alongside two metal hangars.

Outside the hangars waited three planes. Two bi-wing Tiger Moths, a Boeing P-26, and, he grinned, a navy blue Lockheed Altair. It no longer mattered what planes might be hiding inside the hangars. He had helped design the steering system of the Altair and made his decision in an instant.

And it didn't hurt that it was the closest of the four.

He crept from the protection of the brush, stepping as quietly as possible to avoid detection. Two more steps and his right foot emerged from the forest onto the flat dirt.

Machine gun fire pelted the strip and he dove for the safety of the forest. Alvarez and his men shouted, but it didn't seem to be directed at him.

When he dared look, he noticed that Domingo and the others weren't looking for him, much less aiming at him. Instead they darted from the openness of the strip to seek cover in the hangars or around the boxes and oil drums, whatever they could use to protect themselves from…

Lanced laughed out loud when the bullets strafed the field again.

Buck Tellonger sat at the controls of one of the Ranger's cargo planes. And, god bless her, Monique San Diablo, the amazing, wonderful headache of a woman who was to blame for his predicament stood in the open doorway, laying down a hailstorm of bullets with a Bren Mark I.

But he almost outlaughed the noise of the gunfire when he realized how Monique was tethered to the inside of the plane.

There, with one arm holding "the other woman" and the other hand gripping the leather strap at the door, stood Betty, dear sweet Betty, her eyes closed and face gritted tight, but right in the middle of the adventure, nonetheless.

"You're one hell of a lucky man, Lance Star," he told himself.

"I wouldn't say that, my friend."

Lance spun in the foliage.

Standing above him, Señor Rafael Alvarez held a rapier scant inches from his neck.

"It seems I no longer need you," Alvarez said as politely as one could make a threat. "It was an honor to know you, even for this brief time."

"My god!" Betty yelled in her ear. "That's Lance!"

"Where?" Monique asked. "Where?"

Betty's arm around her waist loosened and pointed at the edge of a forest not far from the runway. Lance lay on the ground, and a man stood above him. The man above him held a sword and waved it at him.

"I see him."

"Who's that with him?"

Monique recognized the man immediately. The same one she had suspected from the start. Rafael Alvarez.

"A dead man."

She raised the Mark I and centered Alvarez' forehead in her sights. Then came the momentary tension in her trigger finger just as she squeezed.

"You're one hell of a lucky man, Lance Star..."

The plane jerked slightly, enough to knock off her aim.

"Sorry," Buck called out from the cockpit. "A shot winged the glass up here."

Monique didn't respond. She instead thanked the god of her mother than Betty had one hell of a grip.

"Did I get him? Where is he?"

"I don't know," Betty said. "I lost sight of him when the plane lurched."

"I don't see either of them anymore."

"Coming back around in just a sec, ladies. Hang on."

Alvarez screamed and went down in a heap. He cursed in Spanish, and Lance didn't wait around long enough to translate. He crawled to his feet and high-tailed it toward the Altair.

"Stop him!" Alvarez yelled, but Buck was winging back their way and Monique's blasting of bullets outshouted him, either that or his men were still too afraid to leave their cover.

Lance considered yelling back "Come and get me," but this wasn't one of those pulp novels Red kept stacked up in the lounge at Star Field. And smartass comments could get you killed around shells made of something other than paper, ink and dreams.

"Get me down there. NOW!" Monique shouted as she slung the Bren over her shoulder. She turned to Betty. "Let me go. I need to get down to Lance."

"Are you nuts? Even I can't let you jump from here."

"I'll be fine. I've jumped from higher."

"Not in a moving plane you haven't." Betty grabbed the waist of Monique's pants and held tight. "Besides, if you jumped now, you'd take me with you, and Lance wouldn't like that, would he?"

"Or I could just use you to break my fall and then nurse Lance through his grief at losing you."

Monique forced a smile and locked her gaze onto Betty. Betty held it for a few moments, then raised her eyebrows. Monique felt the grip around her pants relax.

"You would, wouldn't you?" Betty asked. Without waiting for an answer, she pushed her palm into the air between them. "But wait and let Buck get close enough for a safer jump. At least do that."

Monique nodded.

Betty shook her head. "You are crazy, aren't you?"

"It's why I'm the best at what I do."

"Second best."

"Secon…oh? Right, between you and me, we'll let Lance believe that. We women know our men prefer to think themselves our betters, don't we?"

Buck brought the cargo plane back around and as low as he could risk it without bumping the ground. Monique readied herself at the open door.

"You're still going to kill yourself," Betty said.

"Then I'm doing you a favor, honey."

"I'm going with you," said Red, stepping beside her in the light of the doorway.

"You're a mechanic, Red."

"Lance is my friend."

"Then let me do my job."

"Listen to her, Red," Betty said. "And mark this day on your calendar because she and I agree about this one."

They said nothing for a moment. Finally Red spoke. "Damn it."

Another few seconds of silence as the plane passed the hard ground of the runway and entered the soft grass of the clearing beyond it.

"Be careful," Betty said. "And don't' think I didn't catch that 'our men' you slipped in there. I assure you Lance is mine and mine alone. Not 'our' anything."

Monique nodded. "We shall see, Betty. Either way, you're one hell of a adversary."

"Damn right." Betty cleared her throat loudly. "Now go save my damn boyfriend."

"As you wish," Monique grinned as much as said. Then she leaped from the moving plane.

The yoke in his hand felt like home. Lance sat in the cockpit of the Altair and felt the rumbling of the plane's engine shake the seat beneath him. He tested the straps that tightened the parachute around his chest and back.

"Remind me to tell Betty we're not going to vacation at the beach this year. I've had enough water to last me for the next decade," he told the plane, barely making out his own voice over the roar.

He glanced behind him and watched Alvarez limp to the closest hangar, a trail of blood leading all the way from the edge of the forest. That Monique was a crack shot. He'd have to remember to thank her.

But he could worry about that when he was airborne.

He smiled and rolled the Altair onto the runway, then sent it rumbling down the full length of the hard dirt and gravel path. Just before running out of room, lifted the plane into the sky and let the airstrip fall away behind him.

It was like opening the front door and stepping inside his own living room.

He smiled.

But only for a minute or two.

A loud racket behind him warned him he wasn't the only plane in the sky. Jerking the yoke toward him, he looped the Altair to get a good view behind him.

Damn. Why couldn't it have been the P-26, or even one of the Tiger Moths, he wondered, anything but the air cannon? And how long had he been unconscious on board Alvarez's yacht to give them time to ship the damn thing to the island and get it in working order again?

Lance patted the controls in front of him. "I'm counting on you, girl." The Altair would have to work harder than she'd been designed and built to do if he was going to out-fly the experimental Navy plane.

He made a full loop, and brought the shaky plane back under control. "Good girl. Hang in there, baby."

Alvarez was just leaving the ground, and would be on him in no time. For all the air cannon's glitches, it was fast as a hornet and twice as mean. It could easily outmaneuver the off-the-line Altair and came equipped with enough firepower to make short work of him.

Not the best of situations.

But Lance knew he still had an advantage over the rich bastard behind him. He knew what the navy blue Lockheed plane would and could do, and how to push it to those limits. And he also knew what the Navy flyer couldn't do.

He grinned.

This was going to fun. Dangerous and stupid as hell, but fun.

He held the yoke back as hard as he could and aimed the Altair toward the highest cloud he could see. He watched the altimeter. Eight thousand feet and climbing. A good bit less than half of the roughly twenty-three-thousand foot service ceiling the plane could hit and hold. If only it could climb faster.

The Navy was airborne and closing the gap way too fast. Lance calmed his racing nerves with a deep breath. Way, way too fast, he thought.

Strafing fire dotted his wings and one or two appeared to scrape the side of the fuselage, but he ignored the bullets. Nothing vital and thank God nothing near the engine.

The air cannon inched closer, growing larger in his view each time he glanced back to gauge the distance.

He smacked the console. "Climb, damn it, climb!" He sighed. "Sorry, old girl, but I need to you go a lot faster, and any time now."

Monique hit the ground and rolled with a practiced rhythm that had become second nature to her; not that it kept her from dislocating her left shoulder. "Remind me not to jump from a moving plane ever again," she said aloud, to no one in particular.

Which is why she jerked to her feet when a voice answered behind her, "I do not anticipate a next time, Señora San Diablo."

"Domingo," she said, spitting the dirt and dust from her mouth as she took in the sight of the Spanish mass of muscles and scars. Behind him stood a thin Chinese man she'd never seen before. "'Fraid I don't know your date. Care to enlighten a lady?"

"You are not a lady in any way I understand the word," he said, not moving other than to let the machete at his side dangle menacingly.

"Perhaps you should ask your Chinese friend to explain it to you then," she said, following the words with a loud laugh that shook loose the rest of the dirty landing from her throat and mouth. "You do know the different between men and women, right, China-man?"

The man surprised her by bowing deeply, but without lowering his eyes to let her escape his gaze. "My name is Yu. It is a pleasure to meet you."

"Enough," Domingo barked. "You will accompany us back to the villa and wait for Señor Alvarez to return."

"Return?!" She spat and stared into the sky, noticing the two planes above her. A standard issue flyer being chased by what she could only assume was the experimental one inside which Lance had begun this adventure. It looked more like a weird cross between a bat and a triangle than any plane she had ever seen. "I missed them both?!" She stamped her foot hard on the dirt, and it sent an eruption of pain through her shoulder. "Damn it!"

Domingo didn't respond. Not verbally. He merely raised the machete into the air between them. Yu extended his arms to reveal a *wakizashi* in each hand.

"So he's up there?" She pointed into the sky.

Domingo nodded. "He will kill the American pilot and then return shortly."

"Then he obviously doesn't understand who he's up against."

"Just another pilot."

"Even *I'm* not just another pilot, and that amazing man up there put me down on the ground like nobody's ever done before." She laughed. "Lance will make *hors d'oeuvres* out of your boss."

Domingo shook the blade then pointed back down the dirt road. "Enough talk. Let's go."

"Mind if I fix my shoulder first?" Without waiting for a response, she grabbed the joint with her right hand and jerked the dislocated shoulder into place. "Damn it!" she yelled. "Okay. Ready."

"Good," Domingo said.

At the academy, she had practiced for months to learn to draw her Mauser C96 Red 9 the way that stage magicians drew cards and hid them from the crowd, sneaky and quiet and fast. And she had never had cause to regret the hours and hours of work. Nor did she now, as she watched time seem to slow down while she pulled the pistol from inside her coat and trained it on Yu's chest.

It shouted twice and when the sound faded, Yu lay dead on the dirt, a 9mm hole where his heart used to pump, bleeding onto his shirt in the front and coloring the dirt behind him.

Domingo glanced at his dead companion, then made an expression that looked to Monique as though he were trying to eat his upper lip.

"Is that supposed to be a smile?"

He said nothing, but instead raised his arm and then his machete spun blade over grip through the air toward her. She fired but no sooner had she pulled the trigger than the blade knocked the gun from her hand and carved deep gashes into her knuckles.

She shrieked and looked up to see the tank of a Spaniard rushing toward her, barely having time to go limp and meet his stomach with the heels of her boots.

Rolling with his force, she sent him flying behind her and kept rolling until she was back on her feet. She spun around and shook the confusion from her head.

Domingo leaned startled against a tree on the side of the airstrip, where he had hit thanks to her dodge and roll. He too shook the stars from his gaze and arched his back for round two.

Monique slid one foot behind her slightly and shifted most of her weight to the ball of the foot in front, her arms bent at the elbows and her fists tightened.

Domingo rushed her, and she swung the back foot around and caught him in the jaw. He went down to one knee but punched her in the kneecap, and she heard and felt a painful crack. As she regained her balance, he leapt to his feet and followed with another punch toward her gut, but she twisted and let the blow pass a breath away from her side as she rolled along his back and landed a powerful elbow into his kidney. He leaned forward, and she backed away two steps to get her balance again.

Domingo stiffened and locked his arms into a stance that made him look like a third-rate boxer on a triple bill. He punched, and she swerved aside, then rammed her knee into his groin. When he doubled over, she followed with another elbow, this time to the back of his neck. There was a satisfying crunch, and she finished the move with another knee targeted to break his nose.

"Bitch!" he yelled, but she didn't stop.

Both of her hands sped forward and popped the giant Spaniard's ears, and only then did she relax and back away for another round.

He rose and tried to balance, wobbling to the left, then right, the left again, and braced himself against a tree for support.

"Enough of this," he said, and coughed up blood.

"Want a few seconds to count your teeth and make sure they're all there?"

"Enough." He tore away his shirt and revealed a large survival knife sheathed under his arm against his side. He clicked open the snap and pulled the shiny blade out and pointed it her way. "Alvarez wants you alive, but I can always tell him you forced my hand."

"Alvarez isn't gonna make it out of the sky alive, Domingo. Trust me on that."

✠

Seventeen thousand feet, and the Navy bird was all but taking a bite out of his tail. Lance knew he had a good six thousand feet of safe flying ahead of him, but he was sure Alvarez didn't know the experimental plane would stall out at about twenty.

The only problem would be living that long.

More gunfire riddled the Altair, and he held fast, ignoring the Swiss cheese that Alvarez was making of his left wing.

"Bring her down, Lance," his opponent's voice crackled over the radio. "You made a very good effort, and you should be proud. There is no shame in losing this battle, my friend."

Lance grabbed the comm. "Ain't lost yet, Alvarez."

"Surely you are in no condition to drag this out, after what we've put you through, and, to be honest, I'd rather not destroy my plane beyond the point of repair."

Lance checked the altimeter. Nineteen thousand. Just keep him talking…talking and not shooting.

"How 'bout we swap? You let me have the air cannon back so I can return it to the Navy, and I give you back this sweet little Altair?"

Alvarez laughed, and the sound came out far creepier than intended, Lance was sure, over the radio static. "I am afraid that I have decided to keep your Navy plane for my own, my friend. It handles, as you Americans say, like a dream."

"For the most part. She's got her issues, just like any bird."

"You Americans. Always referring to your possessions as women. I wonder what that says about your appreciation of the fairer sex." He laughed again. "And you said that I prefer to own things. I wonder if we are not so very different after all."

"God, I hope not."

More laughter. "Enough talk. Land the plane and I will spare your life long enough to kill you painlessly later."

Twenty thousand feet.

"Got a better offer than that?"

Twenty thousand, two hundred.

The Altair engine began to sputter.

Not good, Lance thought. I made the mistake of assuming he took care of his planes.

⊣⊢

"What's going on out there, Buck?" Betty yelled. "Turn this thing around and get us back down there."

"I'm getting you safe," the older man replied. "You know Lance can take care of himself, and whether you can stomach the Saint Devil or not, she's certainly more than able to handle that action."

"I don't care if…"

"I'm getting you safe," he repeated. "You know Lance would want that."

"I'm not made of porcelain, Buck. I can take care o…"

"I know you can. Not arguing that."

Betty clammed up and stared out the open cargo door. In the distance, way above them, the air cannon had Lance and the warplane dead to rights, and all that machine gun fire sure seemed to be taking its toll. The Altair was already smoking like a Christmas ham.

Down below, Monique and someone else seemed to be little more than ants wrestling over a crust of bread.

Betty slammed her open palm against the wall of the cargo plane. "Hang in there, Lance," she whispered.

She slapped the wall again.

"I feel so useless up here," she said. "I need to be helping them."

"How?" Red asked from the front of the plane, where he had taken over the co-pilot seat. "You've already done what you can, Betty. Now let the professionals do what they do best."

Above them the air cannon closed the distance. She didn't even bother to look down.

"So damn useless."

Domingo's punch knocked loose a tooth. Monique felt something bounce from one side of her jaw to the other and hoped it was only the acrylic fake that had replaced one of the few she had already lost at work. A dame could only take so many blows to the face and still keep her pearly whites.

"That hurt," she said as she shook the pain from her face, and something wet and thick that tasted like iron seeped across her tongue. "Didn't your mother teach you never to hit a lady?"

"A lady? Ha."

"No need to get personal."

Domingo raised the knife, holding the blade between his thumb and forefinger.

She watched for the twitch of her wrist and that gleam in his gaze.

Lance climbed as the Altair engine coughed its last.

Luckily, behind him, the Navy bird had finally caught the same cold.

"Just a few seconds more," he coaxed the plane. "Hang on that long for me, please."

But could it? The warbird had taking a beating thanks to the air cannon's machine guns, and why he hadn't gone down already he didn't know. Dumb luck of the good guys in the white hats, he guessed. The universe looking out for the pure and noble, perhaps. He laughed. A good guy maybe, but nobody was pure and noble. Well, maybe Betty.

"Don't black out," he told himself.

He checked his arms and legs and stomach for wounds. Nothing. That, at least, was something to be thankful for.

Pressure slammed him forward, and he braced himself against the control panel.

The plane fell, tilting back, his nose aiming toward the ground.

The air cannon followed.

"Hey, Alvarez."

"Lance Star," the voice crackled. "It appears we are to die together today."

"Giving up already?"

"You'll never get that Altair engine started again. It was already *muerto* before you took off. I'm surprised you made it this far, whereas I…"

"Whereas you are flying a plane I helped design, and I can tell you that once that engine conks out, it'll take a mechanic to get it turning over again, so unless you want to crawl out onto the front…"

"Touché, Lance. Well played."

"Thanks."

"See you on the ground, and we'll finish this."

Lance laughed. He knew something Alvarez didn't.

He knew he had used the Navy plane's only parachute when he went down days ago.

And when they hit two-thousand feet, Alvarez would have one hell of a surprise.

"Happy landings, Alvarez."

Lance readied his hand on the hatch release.

The blade cut the air beside her, and hissed like a snake in her ear as Monique dove. She hit the ground already in a roll and regained her footing in time to brace for impact when Domingo's larger form slammed into her.

But she was ready for him, falling away as she had done before, letting his force carry them both back and using the momentum to send him sprawling through the air behind her.

She heard the thud, and pushed herself quickly to her feet and spun to brace for another attack.

But it didn't come.

Domingo rested against a tree, but instead of pushing off to rush her, he stood bleeding from a hole in his chest. A broken limb stuck out a good six inches and he held it in both hands.

He coughed blood and tried to speak, but she couldn't make out the words.

She stepped closer.

"Hurts," he whispered, along with something else she couldn't understand, something that sounded like a combination of drowning and drinking at the same time.

He pointed at something behind her on the ground.

She turned and saw the machete where it had fallen after destroying her Mausser.

He nodded.

She grabbed the blade and approached him.

He nodded again, the question of mercy wet in his eyes.

"No." She shook her head, then walked away, carrying the machete with her. "I'm fresh out of mercy today."

Lance was still a few hundred feet from the ground when the air cannon exploded in the island forest. The force shook him and rattled him a bit. He'd have one hell of a headache for the flight home to Star Field.

Below him, Monique waited at the end of Alvarez's runway, waving at him with what he could only assume was some kind of long knife. He guessed she'd done okay with the Spaniard's men.

The cargo plane buzzed above him. He figured the tiny spot looking out the open door had to be Betty. Good ol' Betty.

The flames from the crash crackled loud enough for him to hear as he floated toward the ground.

He closed his eyes.

He'd have one hell of a time explaining all this to the Navy. But he'd rather face that any day than having to get stuck between Monique and Betty inside a cargo plane for the long ride back to U.S. airspace.

In his mind, he was already fixing the design problems for the air cannon.

He felt the ground say hello to his feet and then felt to the dirt repeat the greeting to his knees.

Monique called to him.

The plane rumbled closer, obviously coming in to land.

He let the chute fall around him, and kept his eyes closed.

With any luck, he could sleep it off.

But he knew better.

THE END

Flying High Again
(With Apologies to Ozzy)

How could I say no to Bobby Nash?

I mean seriously, it's like he's my brother from another mother to borrow from the vernacular these days. We travel to and from conventions together, share the pages of more than a few anthologies together, and bounce ideas back and forth off each other all the time. So how could I say no?

I should have checked my calendar and then maybe I could have done it.

As it is, mine is the voice that dragged this little volume of high-flying stories out and made it take so long. Still, I'm glad that Bobby singled me out for taking another flight with Lance and his crew. In volume 3, I was able to take the aviator adventurer out of his plane for a bit and hide him in underground Paris (risking the ire of aviator fiction fans everywhere, I'm sure), and in doing so, I was able to pair him up with a femme fatale of my own creation named Monique San Diablo.

So when Bobby asked me about contributing to another volume, the first thing I asked him was if I could revisit the odd couple pairing of Lance and Monique again.

Luckily, he said yes. If only he had known my devious plans. (Yes, I'm wringing my hands like a Bond villain at the moment.)

And that was that. I knew the minute I finished the previous story that when I ever got to play in Lance's world again I wanted to put Monique and Betty together to have to rescue the man they both palpitated for. I knew that Monique needed to see the bond between Betty and Lance, but that being The Saint Devil, it wouldn't matter to her anyway.

So I took the low road again and this time, instead of taking Lance and shoving into some dirty old catacomb, I dunked him into the ocean after a crash in an experimental Navy plane. I don't know what it is about me having to take the aviator out of the sky for a while. (But don't fear, the absence is what makes Lance's heart grow fonder, as readers will discover, for Lance is, after all, a pilot and does his best work behind the yoke of a plane.)

Then I tortured him. Bad torture. The kind of stuff that would close down Gitmo and impeach presidents. The kind that only real sadists could actually do to someone. (These aren't spoilers. This is opening paragraph trust. It only gets worse for him from there.)

But luckily for Lance, he's got the ladies in his corner.

And that's the story that I had to tell, how one hero could inspire others to be heroic. How one unselfish man could make a very selfish woman do something dangerous in order to save someone else. How one rather non-adventurous woman could become an action hero to try to save the man she loved. And how at the center of all that was the one man who could help foster something amazing in each of them.

Thinking about it that way almost makes it sound like a religious experience, and to some degree (at least for me anyway), all good fiction is. A good pulp action story gets in our heads and changes us for the better, either by encouraging and inspiring the good or by showing us how chooses the bad can lead down a bitter and tragic path with awful consequences.

Maybe that's why I like being a part of Lance's writing bullpen so much. Not only does the high-flying hero inspire his companions. He inspires me too.

Special thanks to Ron Fortier for not killing me when I turned a story in very late. Thanks to Bobby Nash for the same reason and for inviting me again in the first place. Star Field is a good place to hang my hat, even for just a season.

Rise above the clouds and be heroes, my friends.

SEAN TAYLOR - is an award-winning writer of stories. He grew up telling lies, and he got pretty good at it, so now he writes them into full-blown adventures for comic books, graphic novels, magazines, book anthologies and novels. He makes stuff up for money, and he writes it down for fun. He's a lucky fellow that way.

He's best known for his work on the best-selling *Gene Simmons Dominatrix* comic book series from IDW Publishing and Simmons Comics Group. He has also written comics for TV properties such as the top-rated Oxygen Network series *The Bad Girls Club*. His other forays into fiction include such realms as steampunk, pulp, young adult, fantasy, super heroes, sci-fi, and even samurai frogs on horseback (seriously, don't laugh), and he has appeared in short story collections alongside such writing heroes as Joe Lansdale and Nancy Collins. However, his favorite contribution to the world will be as the writer/editor who invented the genre and coined the term "Hookerpunk."

For more information (and mug shots) visit www.taylorverse.com.

Áfterword

AIRBORNE AGAIN

Welcome Loyal Airmen, to this, our fourth volume of adventures featuring Lance Star, Sky Ranger. Publishing little known classic pulp heroes has always been a hallmark of Airship 27 Productions and when we first launched this series we had no idea how Lance would be received by you, the readers. Obviously you liked him and his Sky Rangers lots more than we dared hope and have continued to clamor for more of their high-flying adventures. Which we are only too happy to bring to you.

Aviation heroes were huge in the heyday of the pulps, keeping in mind that the pulps flourished mightily in the 1930s and many of the people who bought those original magazines were themselves World War I veterans who had witnessed first hand the impact of aerial warfare over the skies of France and Germany. They remembered the names of Eddie Brown, the Canadian ace and his opposite number, the flamboyant Manfred von Richtofen; better known as the Red Baron.

The 1930s was a decade of daring barnstorming pilots and amazing advances in aviation technology. Better and faster aircrafts were rolling off the runways of manufacturing plants around the country and it seemed every day a new speed or altitude record was being smashed.

And the pulps were not about to be left out, what with G-8 & His Battle Aces, Bill Barnes, Dusty Ayers, the Gryphon, the Three Mosquitos and dozens upon dozens of other flamboyant flying knights of the sky. Fans just couldn't get enough of their tales of derring-do.

Today, we at Airship 27 Hangar HQ still feel that same adrenalin rush every time we see a plane soar overhead and watch the latest version of lighter-than-air ships sailing across the clouds. We love all manner of airship and are thrilled to be brining you the latest exploits of Lance Star and his faithful team; Buck Tellonger, Cy Hawkins, Jim Nolan and Red Davis. So goose your fuel lines, spin the props of your Skybolts and Skeeter and prepare yourself for take off. Writers Bobby Nash, Sean Taylor, Andrew Salmon and Jim Beard have delivered a quartet of fast paced, high soaring thrills to keep you buckled up tight.

Yes, indeed, Loyal Airmen, we are airborne again!!!

Ron Fortier
3/17/2014
Fort Collins, CO
(www.airship27.com)
(Airship27@comcast.net)

Airship
27

HATS OFF TO THE SERIAL CLIFFHANGERS

The time is 1935. After a decade of fame as the Queen of the Serials, Hollywood actress Gloria Swann is dismayed to see her box-office numbers dwindling with each new production. Desperate to reclaim her popularity, she bankrolls her own film project; an over the top jungle adventure to be shot on location in the wilds of the Amazon rainforests of Brazil.

After the crew and cast arrive at their isolated destination, a series of accidents occur threatening the lives of several of the players. The main target of these unexplained mishaps is Swann's younger stunt double, Angela Morgan. She suspects there are evil forces lurking in the jungle that threaten their safety. Her only ally in this belief is veteran stunt coordinator Karl Braun. When Gloria Swann mysteriously disappears, Angela may be the only hope the Queen of Escapes has to survive.

Writer Curtis Fernlund's homage to the classic film serials of yesterday is a rousing, fast paced adventure that speeds from one danger-filled cliffhanger to the next. James Lyle provides marvelous interior illustrations and Andy Fish captures all the fun in his gorgeous cover painting, packaged and designed by Rob Davis.

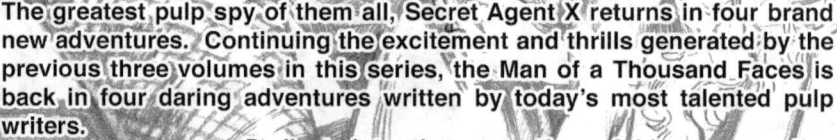